SUPERB WRITING
TO FIRE THE IMAGINATION

Louise Cooper writes: 'When I was little, one of my favourite games was to walk around the house holding a mirror angled towards the ceiling, and trying to navigate by the reflections I saw in it. I found the strange, reversed and upside-down world inside the glass endlessly fascinating, and often made up stories about the people and places that I might encounter there, if I could only reach inside.

I haven't played the mirror game for years, but the worlds of my books still have a lot in common with that long-ago fantasy. They and the mirror images are like borderlands between dreams and reality, and it's in those borderlands that I find inspiration when I write. I'll often look at some everyday scene or object or event, and think: If *this* or *that* aspect were changed, just a little, what new and strange tale might be told then? And so another story starts to take form.

The mirror sculpture that holds the key to Angel's adventures is very like those tracks of thought. Perhaps the worlds within it are a fantasy . . . but then again, who knows what new realities we might find, if w̲   ly turn the key and open the door? T̲   g that it's possible will
And I don't think th

MIRROR

LOUISE COOPER

Hodder
Children's
Books

a division of Hodder Headline

First published in 2000
by Hodder Children's Books

10 9 8 7 6 5 4 3 2 1

A Catalogue record for this book is available from
the British Library

ISBN 0 340 73982 7

Typeset by Avon Dataset Ltd, Bidford-on-Avon, Warks

Printed and bound in Great Britain by
Clays Ltd, St Ives plc

Hodder Children's Books
A Division of Hodder Headline
338 Euston Road
London NW1 3BH

Therapets get everywhere.
So this is for some more of the *real* ones whom
I've met while writing the story —
The felines Ziggy, Sukie, Thomas Grey,
George & Mildred, and Tigger,
And the canines Schooby, Lassie, Barney (1),
Barney (2), Buster, Holly and Ben

ONE

The whirligig homed in, manoeuvred itself until it was spinning directly above the crib, then uttered a racketingly loud bleep.

'WAKEUP, WAKEUP TO YOOOU!' The whirligig was set to Ultra-Positive, and its voice flooded the room with cheerfulness. 'GOOD *MORNING*, ANGEL! THE TIME IS OH-EIGHT-HUNDRED-THIRTY, AND THIS IS YOUR WAKEUP CALL FROM NATURE'S KISSES, BRINGING *YOU* A HEALTHY START TO ANOTHER FULFILLING DAY! NATURE'S KISSES – THE BREAKFAST THAT REALLY *CARES*!'

As the whirligig chirped out its message, a snake of coloured lights flickered along the length of the crib and the soothing purple thru-plast cover turned first to violet then to pale blue and finally became transparent. Angel was curled inside, knees drawn up under her chin and one arm over her face. She was pretending to be asleep, but the light-code on the crib indicated that she was in fact wide awake and listening. The whirligig bleeped again and the window-shades whumped aside, letting in a drizzle of gloomy grey daylight. Another bleep and the grey reality was immediately replaced by a shimmering fake rainbow of gold and blue.

'WAKEUP, WAKEUP, ANGEL,' sang the whirligig.

'WAKEUP TO NATURE'S KISSES, WHO BRING YOU THIS MORNING CALL—'

'Go away!' Angel's voice, muffled by the crib cover, interrupted grumpily.

'CAN'T DO, ANGEL. WAKEUP HAS PRIORITY OVER ALL OTHER COMMANDS.'

With a flurry Angel uncurled herself and sat up, the crib-cover sliding away as she did so. 'Oh, *pigs!*' she said. 'That's not *fair!*'

The whirligig, which was now hanging in the air about two armslengths above her head, bounced agitatedly and turned a sickly green.

'UNDESIRABLE,' it chirruped. 'SOHO DOES NOT APPROVE OF SWEARING.'

'Then pigs to Soho, as well!' Angel shouted back furiously. 'I didn't ask to be woken at this hour, so she can't complain if I swear about it!'

'THE TIME IS OH-EIGHT-HUNDRED-THIRTY. THAT'S NOT EARLY.' The whirligig changed colour again and bleeped twice more as it processed what she had said. 'YOU HAVE BEEN IN SLEEP MODE FOR NINE HOURS FIFTY-FOUR AND SHOULD BE FULLY REFRESHED. IF YOU ARE NOT, IT MAY BE THAT YOUR DEEP-SLEEP PERIOD WAS INSUFFICIENT. SYNERGYMED RECOMMENDS DEE-SEVEN-STROKE-EIGHTEEN, ONE AMPOULE, TO BE REPEATED ONCE BUT ONLY ONCE IF SYMPTOM PERSISTS.' A pause. 'SHALL I PROGRAMME THE DOSAGE TO ACCOMPANY YOUR NATURE'S KISSES BREAKFAST?'

'No,' Angel growled. She knew perfectly well why she hadn't slept properly, and all the doses of D7/18 in the world wouldn't make any difference. It had been another of her headaches; a real banger this time, starting in the back of her skull and then blazing over her eyes. She'd tried six different pills to stop it, then when they failed had tried to distract herself with Hypnos, but even when she set the crib to make her think she was rocking gently on a calm, moonlit sea, accompanied by her favourite subliminal music, she couldn't distract herself from the pain. At one point it had been so bad that she had started crying, and once she started she hadn't been able to stop for ages. Well, pigs *and* flackers to it; she'd use it to her advantage if she could. Today she was supposed to trail along to Interact instead of just having Vee-schol at home. She hated Interact; Vee-schol was easy to skip if you knew how to hack the programme, but with Interact you actually had to be *there*. This might be a good excuse to get out of it, if Soho could be persuaded.

She glared up at the whirligig. 'I don't want any doses of anything. There's nothing wrong with me.'

The bright, spinning globe bounced in the air again. 'JUST GROUCHY, ANGEL? THEN HERE'S TODAY'S HAPPYTHOUGHT FROM THE HAMAMOTO-EMPATHY CORPORATION.' The bedroom walls suddenly came to life, displaying images of smiling, pink-and-gold cherubs fluttering in a sunlit sky, and to a background of cheerful music the whirligig continued, 'HAMAMOTO HAPPYTHOUGHTS TURN DARKNESS TO LIGHT AND GLOOM TO

CHEER, WITHOUT THE NEED FOR MEDICAL AID. AND TODAY'S HAPPYTHOUGHT IS—'

But Angel had had enough. Before the Happythought could be delivered, her fingers moved to the remote-control strip implanted in her left forearm. She flipped the strip on, and as it lit up she touched in the *Commercials Off* code. The music faded, the cherubs vanished from the walls and the whirligig stopped in mid-sentence. Then it burped, its spin wobbled a little, and it said, 'ACCEPTED. BUT SOHO WILL NOT BE PLEASED. I AM AN EXPENSIVE FACILITY, AND COMMERCIAL SPONSORSHIP OFFSETS THE COST OF—'

Angel interrupted. 'Oh, for Tokyo's sake, Soho can afford to shut the sponsors off for a while if she wants to! I don't want a Happythought. I just want some peace and quiet.'

'I REALLY MUST ADVISE—' the whirligig began.

'Don't. Or I'll switch you off, too.' Angel raised her left arm and pointed meaningfully to the control strip. 'This is my birthday present from Soho. It's the new model, and I haven't had a *proper* chance to try it out yet.'

'YOUR BIRTHDAY ISN'T FOR ANOTHER EIGHT DAYS.' But the sphere's tone had changed; it sounded sullen, and just a little uneasy.

'I know. But SynergyMed couldn't give me an appointment then, so I had the fitting done yesterday.' She brandished her arm again, then suddenly and unexpectedly felt a pang of utter misery. Squashing it down – she didn't want the 'gig to register it – she spun round, away from the sphere. 'I want to be left alone. Switch me to house console, then spider off.'

4

'THAT IS ANOTHER SWEAR WORD. SOHO DOES NOT APPROVE—'

'Soho won't know, unless you tell her. And if you do, I promise I'll wipe your antigrav programme and drop you out of the nearest window. It's a *very* long way down. Now, do what I want and *go away*!'

The 'gig hummed, then suddenly the house console in one wall of the room blinked into life. A sulky voice said, 'CONSOLE ACTIVE. DON'T FORGET YOUR BREAKFAST,' and the 'gig drifted across the room and out through the exit-panel. Angel waited for a few moments, until she was sure that the 'gig had really gone, then with a heavy sigh she moved to the console. The food icon was flashing, telling her that her breakfast was ready and waiting, but she ignored the signal and instead considered how she would present herself to her mother.

'Mirror.' She spoke the command and the console screen showed her own reflection. Tokyo, but she looked awful! Her black hair hung in ratty strands and the colours of her last face-make had all worn off, leaving her skin pasty and with huge dark shadows under her eyes. Well, the worse she looked, the easier it would be to convince Soho that she wasn't fit enough to go to Interact. As for clothes . . . better if she didn't bother to dress at all. With luck, appearing in her sleep suit would give the impression that she was too weak to change. That should do it.

She flicked on the console's visual and said, 'Input: house communications. Angel here.'

The house computer's soothing voice came back. 'RECOGNISED, ANGEL.'

'Connect me to Soho.'

'CAN'T DO, ANGEL. SOHO IS OUT OF HOUSE RANGE.'

'Out of . . .' Angel bit back what she had been about to say; she could intimidate the 'gig into not reporting her bad language, but the house computer was another matter. 'Where is she?'

'HOLD . . .' Lights danced on the console. 'MESSAGE WAITING, SOHO TO ANGEL. SHALL I RELAY?'

'Yes, yes.' Where was she, for Tokyo's sake? Then the computer spoke again.

'MESSAGE FOLLOWS.' Abruptly the voice changed to Soho's silvery tones. 'Angel, I'll be in London for the next few days. Kim's in Europe on a short visit and we're going to spend a bit of time together. I'm so sorry I couldn't tell you myself, darling, but it was all arranged in such a rush and it seemed a shame to wake you up just for that. Anyway, I'll be back before your Great Day, so don't worry.' The voice changed again. 'MESSAGE COMPLETE.'

London. Angel felt sick with anger. Soho had *promised* to take her on her next London trip. But Soho's promises had all the substance and durability of a bubble, and as usual she had let Angel down. What made it worse still was that Kim, Angel's father, was going to be there too. Angel hadn't seen him for . . . she counted on her fingers . . . six years? Five, anyway. Kim lived in Beijing, and although they kept in touch through the international Vee-net, Vee wasn't the same as actually being with him. Now he was in Europe – in London, even – and Soho had left her behind while she went to see him alone.

Angel bit her lip hard as she felt tears prickle her eyes. Why was Soho always so selfish? She didn't really care about Kim; they'd only been Paired for two years in the first place and hadn't even renewed once, after the time was up. By the time Angel was old enough to toddle, the Pairing was completely over. All Soho wanted now was to indulge in a bit of nostalgia, and she didn't want Angel around to watch.

But then, Angel thought, what about Kim himself? Their last Vee had been only two weeks ago, and he hadn't said anything then about his visit. In fact he'd told her that he would be hectically busy for a while and might not be in touch. But he must have known he was coming, surely? Or if he didn't know then, he'd have called her to tell her as soon as the trip was arranged?

Perhaps that's it, she told herself bleakly. *Perhaps neither of them wants me hanging around. After all, I'm just their daughter, aren't I? I'd just get in the way and spoil their fun.*

Suddenly her eyes blurred, and the tears she had been holding back poured down her face, hot and stinging. She didn't really know why she was crying, or at least she pretended to herself that she didn't. Must be the after-effects of the headache; she had cried in the night, after all. Yes, yes; that was it. Just the headache. Nothing else. What did she care if she wasn't with Kim? Vee was as good as a real meeting anyway; all right, there was a tiny time-lag, but it didn't give the game away if you pretended hard enough. Flackers to it. Let Soho and Kim have a good time without her. She didn't need either of them.

Angel grabbed a handful of Cloudex from the dispenser and smeared it over her wet face. The tears dried and the Cloudex dissolved, leaving a faint, sickly-flowery smell, and Angel cleared her throat and turned again to the house console. It would have been easier and quicker to use her Personalink (everyone was assigned a Personalink number at birth and kept it throughout their lives) to contact Soho, but Angel was only allowed incoming calls on hers, since she'd run up a huge bill which Soho was still paying off. So she scowled at the screen (why did she always feel that the spidering thing was watching her, like an extension of her mother? It was only a machine!) and said sharply,

'Input: network communications.'

'VEE OR VID?' the computer inquired.

'Vid.' Angel didn't want her mother to look at her too closely. 'Connect me to Soho's Personalink.'

'DO YOU HAVE THE PERSONALINK NUMBER?'

'No.' Angel could never remember numbers.

'HOLD . . . NUMBER FOUND. CONNECTING.' The screen went blank. 'INPUT: ANGEL TO SOHO, VID NETWORK. DO YOU ACCEPT?'

The logo of Eurocomme Corporation flashed briefly across the screen, then it cleared and Soho's three-dimensional face stared out at her daughter.

'Angel?' Soho was obviously in the middle of dressing – she looked vague and distracted and not very pleased. 'What do you want, darling? Didn't you get my message?'

'Yes. But I need to talk to you.'

Soho sighed. Behind her, Angel could see the contours

of a hotel room. It looked very anonymous, all pastel colours and water-walls, like something out of a glossy vid-ad. 'Darling, if it's about my not taking you to London—'

'It isn't that, it's—'

Soho wasn't listening. '—I really *am* sorry, Angel, but it just wasn't practical this time. I know I promised, but this was all arranged at the last minute, and it is mostly business so you'd have been terribly bored stuck here in the hotel on your own. And Kim's schedule is *so* crammed, there really wouldn't have been time to—'

'*Mother!*' Angel interrupted.

The flow of words stopped and Angel watched Soho's beautiful face change to become sharp and angry. Ah. *That* had got to her.

'Angel, you know I don't like you calling me that,' Soho said coldly. 'It's old-fashioned and offensive and silly.'

'I'm sorry, Soho. But you wouldn't *listen.*'

'Well, I'm listening now. What was it you wanted?'

'It's . . . it's about Schol, Soho. I'm supposed to go to Interact today, but last night I . . . I had a terrible headache. It kept me awake half the night, and even Hypnos didn't work, and now I'm *so* tired. Soho, could you sanction me to miss Interact? Just this once?' She paused. 'I'll do Vee-schol instead, I promise.'

The face on the screen loomed closer as Soho peered harder at her. 'You look dreadful. Another one of those headaches, did you say? Well, darling, I don't think it's a good idea to miss Interact, do you? Listen, I'll tell you what; I'll vid SynergyMed and ask them to get someone

9

to come over to Interact and take a look at you while you're there.'

Angel's hopes crashed around her ears. 'Oh, but Soho—'

'Don't argue with me, Angel. You really should go. After all, the headache might be something serious, mightn't it? And if it is, we want to make sure it's nipped in the bud. No, darling, it wouldn't be at all wise of me to let you stay at home, not unless I asked SynergyMed to make a house call, and you know how expensive that is. Now listen, I *must* go—'

'Is Kim there?' Angel cut in.

Soho hesitated. 'He's busy at the moment, darling. Dressing. But he says hello and sends his love. Look, I *must* rush, Angel. I'll call you tonight and see how you got on. Now, you'll take good care, won't you? And don't worry, I'll get in touch with SynergyMed. 'Bye for now!'

Before Angel could reply, the Eurocomme logo danced across the screen again and Soho was gone.

'DURATION OF CALL,' the computer said, 'ONE MINUTE FORTY-EIGHT SECONDS. CALL LOGGED OH-EIGHT-HUNDRED-FIFTY-FOUR, STANDARD VID TARIFF. THE EURO-COMME CORPORATION THANKS YOU FOR YOUR INPUT AND WISHES YOU A FULFILLING DAY.'

With a great effort Angel resisted the reply she wanted to make, and, shoulders drooping, got to her feet. She should have known it would be useless. Soho simply wouldn't let her miss Interact for anything, not after the last report she had had from Cray, her Experience Incentive Leader. Cray hadn't exactly *said* that Angel was anti-societal, but the implication was clear that, unless she pulled herself together and became more outgoing, her future prospects didn't look good. Soho had thrown a fit. Didn't Angel care about what she might become? Did she want to waste her life, perhaps end up in the streets, unprotected and uninsured, easy prey for one of the marauder gangs or, worse, initiated *into* such a gang; a hopeless drop-out, sick in body and mind and – here Soho had paused for dramatic emphasis – *doomed*?

Angel wanted no such thing. She knew all about the marauder gangs who roamed and virtually ruled the streets, and was terrified of them. She also knew what happened to people who didn't have proper medical care; the diseases, the premature ageing, the *decay*. She wasn't so stupid as to let that happen to her, and Soho knew it. But Soho pretended she didn't know, and used Cray's report at every opportunity to make sure that Angel didn't step out of line. Which, in Angel's story-vid, was pure emotional blackmail.

Angel stared at the house console screen, which now showed a moving mandala of soft colours that was supposed to be soothing. It didn't soothe her in the least, so she mouthed the rudest word she could think of – very quietly, so the computer wouldn't hear and report it to Soho – and made a gesture which the console could interpret however it pleased. Then she swung round and looked about at her surroundings. The big window, programmed by the 'gig, twinkled its blue and gold rainbows at her, filling the room with pleasant light. Angel curled her lip and touched the control strip in her arm. She didn't want to be seduced by the 'gig's idea of what a morning should be; she wanted to see what the weather outside was *really* like. There was a sigh from the window, the rainbows blurred together and vanished, and a square of dreary grey shot through with sullen and murky purple confronted her. Ah. Fog *and* rain. No wonder the 'gig hadn't wanted her to see the outside world. But it suited her mood to perfection.

She moved back to the console. What did she feel like wearing today? Something sombre, she decided, with a touch of tragi-drama. The screen started to trawl through images of her clothes, and the soft wardrobe voice whispered ingratiatingly, 'To make you feel *really* good on this lovely day, Angel, why not choose purple and pink, with just a *hint* of silver, to flatter your natural good looks and make sure that you are noticed wherever you go? I would recommend—'

'Terminate!' Angel interrupted through clenched teeth. Soho had been meddling with the programme again: she *adored* purple and pink and was always trying to get Angel to wear them. Angel, naturally, loathed them both. Instead, she decided on the oldest, best-loved and most thoroughly unSoho item in her wardrobe: a single-piece swirlsuit that covered her from throat to ankles. Soho said it was shapeless and dowdy, it swirled in all the wrong places and she looked appalling in it, but for nearly six months now it had been Angel's favourite, and she ordered it from the cubicle. When it appeared, she toned the interactive fabric to black and grey, and chose a pair of heavy black skimmer boots to match. With a black hoodcape to complete the picture, she would make an ideal match with the outside world.

Angel smiled a grim and very private little smile, and began to prepare herself for the day ahead.

TWO

Angel took the public String to the Experience Mart, where Interact was held. She hated the journey, but Soho wouldn't allow her to hire an auto ('Angel, the *expense*! And anyway, darling, we live in Zone Bohemia; it's *expected* of people like us to use the String'). So instead of descending just a couple of floors to Azure Block's autonet link, she had to go all the way down to ground level, face the short but unpleasant outdoor walk to the nearest String access, wait for a cylinder and then share it with Tokyo alone knew how many other people, all squashed in together and breathing each other's used air. The public String could be frightening, too. Marauders hung around at the accesses, and though there were always Vigilants on patrol to stop any real trouble, *they* could be as unpleasant in their own way as the gangs. Angel hated the way the Vigilants *stared*. They all seemed to have extraordinarily small, muddy-coloured eyes, and their gazes bored into her as though they were waiting and hoping for her to make one wrong move, to give them an excuse to pounce.

There were two Vigilants at the access when she arrived, both men with faces grey and unhealthy from outdoor work and unpleasant-looking stains on their scarlet uniforms. Angel didn't smile at them – there was no point, they never smiled back – but spoke her name, destination and purpose at the host-holo, waited for her voice-print to be checked, then, shoulders hunched, hurried into the thru-plast tunnel. She was relieved when the aperture closed behind her and the conditioners replaced the stink of the outside world with laundered air. Though today's Thematic Essence – which according to the singing adstrip on the tunnel wall was 'Hearts In Paradise' – made her feel nearly as sick. There were six or seven people waiting for the next cylinder. One tall, thin and unhealthy-looking man gave her a raking stare but then looked away, and Angel was thankful that she had chosen grey and black for her clothes, and a face-make to match. Last Interact, Soho had told her that she should dress more flamboyantly – another result of Cray's report – and she had been followed all the way to the Experience Mart by some spidering old creep with a sparkle-eye transplant, who kept calling after her and then bursting into high-pitched giggles. It wasn't an experience she was anxious to repeat.

The cylinder arrived at last and the passengers all piled in. By pushing, Angel managed to get a seat near the aperture, and as the cylinder started to move she shut the supposedly relaxing music out of her mind (she *hated* that spidering music!) and lapsed into her favourite daydream, the one she'd programmed into her own Vee at home. In it she wasn't Angel Ashe of Azure Block, Zone Bohemia, Birmingham, Eurostate 8, but Angel Ravenhair of the Crystal Tower, Mistress of Sorcery, Lone Warrior of Light, riding on her snow-white horse across the misty wastes of Avalonne to challenge the Lords of Darke in eternal struggle. Angel didn't know whether there still were any real horses; certainly when she'd been very little and Soho had taken her to the Cultural Nostalgia Gardens she couldn't remember seeing one. But in the world of Vee she could have any kind of horse she wanted. Other animals, too; not automaton Therapets like some of her co-educationates had (and Soho wouldn't let her have, because 'it would get under my feet all the time, darling, and the noise they make is *so* distracting,') but true-life ones that needed feeding and had real fur to touch and stroke. In her Avalonne she had anything she wanted; spells to make her fly, a Crown of Power, her crystal wand with which she could read the truth in the hearts of friend and foe alike. And above all, she had Winter. She called him Winter because he was strange and cold and dangerous, the way winter apparently used to be long ago. His skin was white as snow – Angel had never actually *seen* snow, because it never snowed in Eurostate 8 any more, and she'd never actually visited any of the countries where it still did. But she'd experienced snow in Vee, and liked it. She now used it to describe many things in Avalonne. Winter's hair was palest gold, and his eyes . . . she could send a flurry of delicious shivers down her spine just *thinking* about his eyes. Dark and deep and filled with bitter sorrow, hiding memories of ancient battles and dreadful griefs, of which he could never speak to another human soul. Winter was Angel's paramour, but their relationship was a stormy one and when they quarrelled Winter would retire to pace the halls of his lonely ice-fortress in the far, far north, while she, courageous in her sadness, donned the Crown of Power once more and rode out on a new and perilous quest.

Nothing in the world would have persuaded Angel to let anyone else into Avalonne. She had never even *told* anyone else about it; it was her secret, her private world, an escape from all the frustrations and disappointments of her life – particularly from Soho and Cray and all the other people who *cared* so much about her but whose caring seemed to have more to do with their needs than with hers. During the last year she had spent more and more of her free time in Avalonne, and she wished she could be there now instead of flying along the String towards another dreary day of Interact . . .

A chiming sound interrupted the music suddenly and thumped her mind back to earth. Angel blinked, and a soothing voice floated through the cylinder.

'WE ARE APPROACHING EXPERIENCE MART GATE ONE. ALL CUSTOMERS FOR EXPERIENCE MART GATE ONE PLEASE BE READY TO DISEMBARK. YOUR CO-OPERATION IS THE GUARANTEE OF OUR EFFICIENCY. THANK YOU FOR TRAVELLING WITH SERENITY STRING SERVICES, AND MAY *YOUR* DAY BE A DAY OF JOY.'

Annoyed by the voice, Angel deliberately took her time in getting out of the cylinder. She could see the aperture straining to close and she blocked it for nearly twenty seconds, secretly hoping that she might blow a superconductor or two and mess up the whole system. It didn't happen, of course – it never did – and at last she stepped down and followed her fellow travellers towards the exit.

Gate One led to the Cultural Enrichment sector of Experience Mart, and as she entered the first of the galleries Angel saw that they had a new art exhibition on the theme of water. A lot of the exhibits had been vandalised by marauders, but some were still working, up to a point, and she hung around for a few minutes to see if there was anything worth watching. Most of it was boring and unimaginative, but a few of the exhibits were actual, *real* sculptures instead of holos or Vees. Angel was intrigued . . . and when she reached the very last exhibit, all thought of Interact flicked straight out of her mind.

It was labelled 'Future Passed' and it stood apart from the other sculptures, at the far end of the gallery where three walkways fanned off to other parts of the sector. For what was in fact only a matter of seconds but seemed to her like half a lifetime, Angel simply stood motionless, staring hypnotised at the kaleidoscope of silver reflections, shot through with eerie shades of blue and green, that seemed to draw her mind in and in and in, as though she were tumbling into a vortex of dreams. A logical part of her knew that there was nothing mystical about it; it was only jets of water cascading over mirrors that had been cleverly placed to create an infinity of reflections. But she pushed the knowledge away, not wanting it to spoil the sculpture's fascinating, captivating beauty and strangeness.

She crouched down to get a better view, and suddenly a face appeared in the heart of the sculpture; a strange, silvery face with huge, dark eyes gazing intently back at her. Angel started violently – then laughed as she realised it was her own reflection, transformed by the mirrors and the water. She looked just like – she smiled with delight at the thought, and the reflection smiled too – just like her secret vision of Angel Ravenhair of the Crystal Tower; elfin and mysterious, and not *quite* human. And if she turned her head just a bit to the left and tilted her chin like *this*, the hidden jewel-coloured lights in the sculpture started to—

The thought collapsed. Because suddenly the face looking back at her wasn't hers, or Angel Ravenhair's, but that of a stranger.

Angel froze, staring. The new image in the mirror was a boy of about her own age. He had pale grey eyes and plain, angular features, and his pale hair looked as if it hadn't been styled, or even cleansed for that matter, for days. He was frowning, and as Angel continued to stare, his mouth moved as though he was muttering something, though there was no sound but for the tinkling of the water cascades.

Then a horrible thought struck Angel. *Perhaps a marauder had crept up behind her, and—*

She spun round, right hand groping for the alarm button on her arm unit, ready to summon the Vigilants. But the gallery was deserted. And when she turned back to the sculpture again, there was the strange boy, still looking, still muttering silently with that frown on his face.

An awful surge of vertigo swept over Angel. The walls of the gallery seemed to topple towards her and she felt her balance going. She was falling forward, falling towards the flowing water and glittering mirrors, and the boy's face was breaking up into thousands of fragments that seemed to explode out at her as blackness rushed up from under the floor to overwhelm and engulf her—

'Lie still and don't try to breathe too deeply, Angel. I'm just going to give you a stimulator shot and then everything will be fine.'

Angel felt a tingling in her right arm, then the world came swimming back out of the darkness as she opened her eyes. She was lying surrounded by the soothing blue walls of a Recovery Cubicle, and two people were looming over her. One was a woman dox with the glowing SynergyMed logo implanted in her forehead; she was smiling. The other was Cray, and he was not.

'There.' The dox dropped the used stimulator into a disposer and reached out to help Angel sit up. 'All better now? Nothing to worry about; you're double-A fit.'

Cray interrupted before Angel could say anything. 'If she's double-A, why did she faint?' he demanded, and Angel saw that the Mood Interpreter jewels in his fingers (they were the latest fashion but Soho wouldn't let her have them) were flashing orange and violet, a sure sign that Cray was very wound up indeed.

The dox shrugged. 'There could be ten reasons, and none of them mean that there's any physical problem.' She drew Cray aside and added something that Angel wasn't meant to hear, though she caught the word *neurotic*. Cray relaxed a bit and nodded knowingly, and Angel fumed.

'I am *not* neurotic!' she said loudly, hoping that her voice would carry through the cubicle aperture because she was pretty sure that all her co-educationates would be out there, straining their ear-muscles to listen. Cray's Mood-jewels turned completely purple (Good! That meant he was *really* hopping mad now) and he swung round.

'That's enough, Angel! Unless you want an Offence mark on your next report?'

Angel knew what Soho would say about another Offence, so she shrugged and shut up. By annoying Cray she had achieved what she wanted anyway.

The dox was packing up her kit. 'I've given her a shot of Neuroeze along with the stimulator,' she said, talking to Cray as if Angel wasn't there, and flipped open her wristband coder. 'If you'll just adult-authorise the callout, I can log the fee to her Prime Parent's account.'

'It's authorised already,' Angel said, not wanting Cray's nose poked any further into her business.

The dox checked the coder and shook her head. 'No.'

'But my m—Soho called you earlier. She told me.'

'No,' the dox said again, sounding impatient now. 'There's no call logged.' She waved her wristband at Cray. 'If you don't mind? I've got other clients to see this morning.'

Cray pressed his thumb on the coder, while Angel sat mute with disappointment and anger. So Soho hadn't even kept *that* promise. She'd probably forgotten all about it the moment the vid disconnected. Too busy having fun with Kim . . .

With a nod and another fake smile to Angel the dox left the cubicle, clicking away on her glass heels. When the aperture shut, Cray turned and gave Angel a very long look. Then he folded his arms and said, 'Well?'

Angel shrugged again, still stinging from Soho's betrayal. 'Well what?'

The Mood-jewels flickered purple again but Cray managed to keep his temper under control. 'What *happened*, Angel? And don't tell me it was marauders, because Security say there haven't been any in Cultural Enrichment Sector this morning.'

He was still looking hard at her and it made Angel uncomfortable. She didn't want to tell Cray the truth, because Cray was so spidering *normal* that even to mention the sculpture at all would soil it somehow. So she turned her head away and put on a meek voice. 'I don't know what happened, Cray. I was looking at the art exhibition and then suddenly I came over dizzy, and I don't remember anything else until I woke up here.'

Cray looked suspicious. 'And there wasn't anyone with you? You were on your own?'

Obviously he thought she had picked up with some 'undesirable' company and was trying to hide it. 'No,' Angel said firmly. 'I told you. There wasn't anyone else around.'

Cray gave her the kind of look that said he didn't believe her but, as he couldn't prove anything, he was prepared to let the matter drop. Very gracious of him, Angel thought.

'Well,' he said, and the Mood-jewels told Angel that he was feeling resentful, 'we'd better get back to Interact. Though of course you've managed to ruin most of what I had planned for today's session with this interruption.'

'I couldn't help it!'

Cray grunted, then stared at her again. 'I understand

that Soho has gone to London, to meet Kim.'

That caught Angel unawares – how could he have known? 'Yes,' she said, suddenly defensive.

Cray nodded. 'Then I expect that was why you were late, wasn't it?' He smiled, and the smile was sly. 'I expect you were worrying about the plans they're making for you. After all, it's your fifteenth birthday next week, isn't it?'

Angel's stomach froze, as if she had swallowed an entire glitter-ice in one mouthful. Soho could only have told Cray about Kim's visit at Education's last Parent Symposium. So the London trip hadn't been a last-minute rush at all. She and Kim must have been planning it for ages, and a miserable feeling of betrayal washed over Angel as she realised what that meant. Next week, as Cray said, she would be fifteen, and so would no longer have to attend Vee-schol. But as to what she would be doing . . . well, that all depended on Soho, because for the next two years, until she reached seventeen and officially became an adult, Soho would have complete control over her life.

That was why Soho was meeting Kim. Legally, Prime Parents didn't have to consult Secondary Parents about the decisions they made, and Angel knew perfectly well that Soho didn't really give a brown rat for what Kim thought or wanted. But at the moment it was terribly fashionable for both parents to 'Share and Relate' about their children, and Soho *always* followed fashion. Between them, then, she and Kim were deciding Angel's future.

Angel knew that Soho could make one of three choices for her. She could put her into Ongoing Ed, or assign her to a Vocation . . . or she could choose Societal Adequacy. In theory, Societal Adequacy was supposed to be a general, all-round Experience of Life, preparing Schol-leavers for adult responsibilities. But in practice, it was a very convenient way for bored Prime Parents to get their children off their hands – because there was another word for Societal Adequacy, and that word was 'Pairing'.

It wasn't that Angel didn't like the idea of getting Paired. In fact she'd often thought about it, and about the fun she and her partner might have in an apartment of their very own, without their Prime Parents to tell them what they could and couldn't do all the time. But when she did Pair, she wanted it to be with someone *she* had chosen, and to do it when *she* was ready. She didn't want the choice to be forced on her. Above all, she didn't want the choice to be made by Soho.

Angel looked at Cray again. He was still smiling that repulsively sly smile at her, and now he was smug, too. Soho had told him what she was planning. Not a word, not a hint to Angel, but she'd told *Cray*. Angel felt sick with fury. Well, if Cray was waiting for her to ask him what he knew, she wasn't going to give him that satisfaction. Besides, she didn't need to ask, because the answer was obvious. Ongoing Ed was expensive, and though Soho had plenty of money she would rather spend it on herself than on anyone else. Vocation meant two more years of Prime Parental responsibility, and that already cramped Soho's style a lot more than she liked. Pairing, then, was the obvious answer. Angel could be shoved into a one- or one-point-five year contract and sent off to live in one of the First Pairing apartment blocks. She would then be out of Soho's hair and, apart from making over a small allowance, Soho could forget all about her. If Angel didn't like it, too bad, because by law, she couldn't refuse.

Angel looked at her long, sparkling black fingernails – new ones she had put on this morning – and wished she had the courage to rake them down Cray's face, for the sheer pleasure of watching that smug look disappear. Instead, though, she gave another shrug and turned towards the aperture.

'I don't need to worry about Soho's plans for me,' she said, hoping that she sounded a lot more carefree than she felt. 'She and I *always* agree. About *everything*.' Looking back over her shoulder she gave Cray an innocent smile, though behind it she was having sweet dreams of murder. 'Now, if you're in such a hurry to get back to Interact . . .?'

She opened the cubicle aperture. And there they were, the twenty-three co-eds of her Experience Incentive group, hanging around outside. Though they tried to look nonchalant they were obviously all agog. Festival Drew even had her ear pressed against the wall; Angel saw it before Festival could jump back. Angel raked them all with a filthy look, which they returned with sneers. Someone, mimicking her own voice, said, 'Ooh, *neurotic!*' Angel tilted her chin, ignoring the jibe, and swept past them, out into the Thematic Essence-scented air of the Experience Mart.

THREE

On her birthday, Angel had two surprises.

Soho had come back from London, dazzling with the latest fashions and with her hair changed from its short, silver curls to a mane of black and crimson stripes. She was full of concern over Angel's health – though she *was* a little annoyed that Angel had refused counselling for her headaches – and promised that when the Great Day (as she insisted on calling it) came, Angel was going to get something very, very Special.

The Great Day didn't start too well. Angel broke the heel of one of her favourite shoes by throwing it at the Whirligig when it insisted on singing a brand-new sponsored wakeup jingle at her, and then over breakfast she found that her co-educationates had logged a string of silly birthday messages on the Vee-net projector. At first they were fun, but after nearly half an hour of holo images of her friends jumping around, pulling hideous faces and cracking awful jokes she had had enough. In fact she was starting to feel like throwing up the plate of Nature's Kisses that she had eaten. Soho, though, pretending it was still hilariously funny, insisted on playing all the messages through to the end. When at last they were over, she gave Angel the first surprise.

It was a Therapet. One of the newest models, a cat with

sparkling golden fur and enormous silver-and-green eyes in an adorable, irresistible face. Soho, hovering, said, 'Kim wanted you to have something extra-special this year, darling, and I feel *just* the same! So this is from both of us.'

Angel stared at the cat, then at her mother. 'But Soho, you've always said—'

Soho interrupted hastily. 'I know what I've said, Angel, but . . . well, this birthday's different, isn't it? Your fifteenth.' She sighed sentimentally, then beamed at Angel. 'Do you like it, darling? Tell me you do!'

Angel did; that was the trouble. Because she knew, she just *knew*, what this meant. It was a sweetener, to soften her up for something else that she wouldn't like one spidering bit. And she didn't need to be the brightest student in Cray's Cognitive Inter-Relation classes to know exactly what that something was.

She felt as if her heart was sinking right down into her stomach and beyond it to her feet. But the Therapet cat was looking at her, and its big eyes were appealing to her . . . 'Yes, Soho,' she said, and there was a funny little catch in her voice. 'It's . . . lovely. Thank you.'

Soho swooped and planted a huge kiss on her forehead. 'I'm so pleased! And Kim will be, too. We *both* want to make you happy!' She dropped down to her knees on the floor beside Angel, and suddenly she seemed about ten years old. 'Let's switch it on, shall we?' She snatched up the cat, turned it to a very undignified upside-down angle and pushed her fingers into the lush fur between its ears to find the activator pad.

There was a peculiar squeaking noise that made the

ever-attendant 'gig respond with a surprised burp, then
the cat wriggled out of Soho's hands, dropped to the floor
on four neat paws, turned itself around and blinked its
irresistible eyes directly at Angel.

'Hello, Angel!' The voice was high-pitched and – Angel
couldn't think of a better word for it – *twinkly*; a cross
between a purr and the sort of syrupy, goo-goo tone that
people used with babies. 'I know who you are. You're Angel,
and I hope that you're going to be my friend.' It blinked
again. 'Will you be my friend, Angel?'

Angel looked at Soho and saw that she was frowning.

'I do hope you'll be my friend, Angel,' the Therapet
said. 'Because, you see, I'm just a little pussy-cat who hasn't
got a home and hasn't got a name. May I come and live
with you, in your home, Angel? And will you give me a
name?'

Soho blinked her gorgeously-enamelled eyes rather
rapidly and said, 'Er . . .'

'Shall we play, Angel?' the Therapet suggested, ignoring
Soho. 'I know a lovely song, all about my sponsors, who
are called Recreation Realm FunFriends. That's a big
name to say, isn't it? But I *know* you'll soon learn it, just
the way I did. Shall I sing my song about Recreation
Realm FunFriends for you now?'

Just in time Angel managed to splutter out, 'No!' and
the Therapet fell silent, looking puzzled. Soho, with a
funny, snorting catch in her voice, said, 'Oh, Tokyo, they've
programmed it to First Level! I told them, I absolutely
told them – but these wretched people never *listen*!'

Angel couldn't help it; she started to laugh, and once

she started she couldn't stop. She laughed at the Therapet's baffled and now faintly indignant expression, she laughed at Soho's efforts to reprogramme the cat (and at the language she used while she was doing it), and when, half an hour later, the house computer gave a soft chime and announced that Kim was calling on the Vee-net Angel was still giggling as she hugged and thanked him – or rather, his Vee projection.

The Therapet, she and Soho at last decided, was faulty, for when they did at last manage to reprogramme it, with some help from the Whirligig, the First Level settings still kept cutting in from time to time. Furious, Soho wanted to vid the Recreation Realm Corporation immediately, give them a piece of her mind and threaten to sue them 'for the damage their mistake might have caused to my child's mental health and stability.' But Angel said no. She rather liked the cat's oddities – they made it different, and she would rather keep it as it was than get another one. Eventually Soho gave in, probably relieved that she wouldn't have to suffer the strain of an argument with Recreation Realm, and Angel named the Therapet 'Twinkle' because of the silly voice it used when it slipped back into little-kid mode. Though nothing would have persuaded her to admit it to anyone, secretly she felt grateful to Twinkle, because quite by accident the little cat's defects had brought her and Soho closer, simply by making them laugh together. For the first time in what felt like ages, and probably was, Soho and Angel were on the same wavelength. That made Angel feel good.

The good feeling, however, was doomed not to last for

long. And it was the party that broke the spell.

'Real Event' parties were a big fashion at the moment, and Soho had been fairly easily persuaded to let Angel have one to celebrate her birthday. A module had been hired at the Experience Mart for the evening, and nearly a hundred guests were invited, including all Angel's Schol friends. Angel spent the afternoon having a new face-make and choosing what clothes to wear, then in the evening, as the city holos began to come on and Azure Block was bathed in imitation moonlight, she and Soho took an autonet car to the Mart. Soho looked stunning in a skinsuit that matched her hair and was trimmed with floaty, feathery streamers, while Angel had chosen gold and silver, face and clothes alike, with a Quikon-Quikoff treatment to turn her black hair to metallic green. As a final touch, she draped Twinkle around her shoulders like an arti-fur collar. She and the Therapet matched perfectly, and although Twinkle's purrs were sometimes interrupted by snatches of baby-talk as the programming glitched again, Angel was rather pleased with the overall effect.

The party was in a penthouse module and the theme was Deep Space; with images of galaxies and nebulae whirling across the ceiling dome. Angel and Soho stepped out of the bubble-lift, and as Angel walked in at the open entrance the semi-darkness inside suddenly exploded into brilliance as a swarm of holo-comets whooshed through the room, and the classic birthday song, 'This Is Your Merry, Merry Day', swirled around her so loudly that the floor shook.

Twinkle's programme went wrong again and the

Therapet started to sing 'I'm Just A Little FunFriend', which clashed horribly, but Angel didn't have time to do anything about it because people were crowding round her wishing her happy birthday, and a Whirligig was towing trays of food and drinks and glitter-ices towards her. Suddenly the party was in full swing.

For the first two hours, Angel had a wonderful time. She danced, ate, laughed, showed off Twinkle to her friends, and was even persuaded to get up in front of the live-music computer and sing two numbers. But at last Soho, who had been dancing as energetically as anyone, pounced on Angel and told her there was someone here she simply *must* meet.

With Twinkle pattering at her heels and skilfully avoiding trampling feet, Angel was led to where a tall, fair-haired man and a boy of about her own age were standing together at one side of the room.

'Darling,' Soho said, 'say hello to York. And this,' she indicated the boy, and later Angel realised that her mother's smile had actually given the game away at that moment, 'is York's son, Bright.'

Angel said hello, not thinking anything more of it at the time. York was hearty, slapping her palm for much longer than necessary and giving her a wink which she didn't understand, and Bright had a drawling voice which instantly irritated her. He said, 'A-hu, Angel. This is a really *screaming* party; I'll tell you, it's just *as*, really just *as!*'

Oh, spiders, Angel thought, *what a fad-radical!* Being fashionable was one thing, but slavish fashion-followers, the kind who spouted all the latest jargon even if it was nine hundred per cent brainless and meaningless, made her ill. She swallowed a diabolical urge to grab a plateful of cakes from the nearest 'gig servitor and push them one by one into Bright's face, and with a vast effort forced herself to smile. 'Hi,' she said.

Soho, who either hadn't noticed her reaction or was determined to ignore it, grabbed her arm and propelled her a step nearer to Bright. 'Angel, York and I have something to talk about, so why don't you and Bright dance?' She beamed at Angel. 'He knows all the latest dance-moves; he's just . . . well, just *as*, isn't that right, Bright?'

'Oh, double-*positive*,' said Bright. Angel, stifling giggles, thought, *I'll throw up. I will. I really will.* But before she could even think about saying no, Bright had caught hold of her hand and was towing her towards the dance area. Finding the best-lit spot he could – in other words, the spot where the maximum number of people could see and admire him – he struck a pose, listened to the beat of the music for a few moments, then pointed both thumbs at his own head.

'Uh, *no*. It's just too un-*me* . . . look, hover a min, Angel, yuh?' He went to the music computer, touched the panel, and suddenly the tempo changed to something much faster and more complicated.

'Oh, *as*!' Bright was back, carefully arranging his hair with one hand. 'Angel, let's turn, yuh?'

They turned. Or rather, Bright did, hopping and gyrating in a world of his own while Angel watched with increasing disbelief. He certainly knew all the latest dance-moves, including a good few which, presumably, were so *as* that Angel hadn't even heard of them yet, and his dancing was punctuated with high-pitched yelps which cut through the music and made everyone turn and stare at him. When, after about ten minutes of energetic cavorting, he finally took a break, he – and Angel could hardly believe this – actually turned and *bowed*, like a character out of a history-fict, to all the spectators, and they actually *applauded*.

Twinkle, by now draped round Angel's neck again, raised her head (Twinkle was a 'her', Angel had decided) and began to trill a song called, 'Little Pink Flowers'. Angel growled, 'Programme terminate!' out of the side of her mouth, and looked desperately around for Soho. But she and York were still talking a little way off. Soho was making up to York now, and Angel realised that her mother fancied him madly, which meant she would be stuck with Bright for a while yet. So she tried to make the best of it and, as Bright returned to her side with a flick of his perfect hair, she said, 'That was . . . interesting.'

Bright smiled and gave another flick of his perfect hair. 'Turning always makes me feel . . . well, y'know how it scans . . . really double-*now*, yuh?'

'Yuh.' Angel loaded the word with sarcasm, but it seemed to fly straight over Bright's head. 'So when you're not being double-now, what else do you do?' she asked.

'Oh, skies, just blue *skies* of things. Like, I spent all last week in Vee, trawling for clothes. Got a complete new wardrobe, and I promise you, it's not just as, it's *pre*-as – ahead of everyone, and I mean *everyone* in the city, let alone Zone Bohemia!' He flicked a glance over Angel. 'You go trawling, yuh?'

'Not much.' In truth, Angel always shopped by vid, for clothes or anything else. If you trawled in Vee you got all those holo-sales creeps almost licking your feet in their efforts to make you buy and telling you how you couldn't possibly live without their products . . . it gave her the crawls.

'Oh, you should!' Bright told her. 'It's just unsur-*passing*! Look, why not trawl with me one of these days? Like I said, I know what's pre-as – I could really help you to make the *most* of yourself!'

That did it. To have to put up with this this – she tried to think of the worst insult she could and came up with something that was swearing on a grand scale – this *frog* was one thing, but to have him stand here and patronise her was more than Angel could stand. She opened her mouth to tell him exactly what she would like to do to make the most of *him*, and—

'Angel, darling!' Like a feathered whirlwind Soho swooped on her, clamping an arm around her shoulders and making Twinkle squawk agitatedly. 'Your horrible, thoughtless Prime Parent has been neglecting you! Come on, come and have something else to drink, and then you can tell me *all* about the fun you're having!'

York was lurking in the background, grinning. Bright said, 'Hover, Angel, yuh? I'll catch your sparkle later!' and Soho waved grandly to them both as she swept Angel away.

At one side of the room, away from the crush, they

34

stopped. 'Well, darling?' Soho said. 'Do you like Bright?'

Angel opened her mouth—

'Isn't he just *as*? And so beautiful and mature; you'd think he was much older than fifteen, wouldn't you?'

Angel opened her mouth again—

'I'm so thrilled for you, darling. For both of you. When York first suggested it I wasn't entirely sure, because I had wondered if it might be better for your development to pair with someone from another Zone, especially for your very first Pairing, but then Kim and I talked it over and he felt . . .'

Soho twittered on but suddenly Angel wasn't hearing the words any more. Her mouth had opened again and this time it stayed open, How could she have been so *stupid*? Everything had pointed to this. First the Therapet, then the lavish party, then Soho pushing her and Bright together, and all the winking and silliness between Soho and York – the hideous truth had been staring her in the face, and she hadn't seen it!

'. . . one of those gorgeous new First Pairing apartments; they've got all the facilities a young couple could ever *dream* of, and there are resident Societal Adequacy Counsellors, so whatever you need to ask, they'll always—'

Angel's voice cut suddenly across hers in an unsteady bleat. 'Soho . . .'

'—be on hand to help, and—'

'*MOTHER*! !'

Heads turned. Soho stopped in mid-sentence and stared. Shaking with fury Angel said, 'Mother, what have you done? Are you telling me you've – you've contracted for me to *Pair* with Bright?'

Soho's eyebrows went up so far that they almost vanished into her hair. She looked pained, and as puzzled as Twinkle. '*We* have, darling, Kim and I. It was a mutual decision. I don't know why you're so surprised – or, quite honestly, why you seem so upset. Bright's an absolute sweetie; you've seen that for yourself. You really couldn't have wished for anyone nicer for your first Pairing!'

Angel started to shake and couldn't make it stop. This wasn't true! It was a dream, a nightmare, it *had* to be! But Soho was smiling at her, and in the background she could see York and Bright, coming towards them like two marauders closing in on their prey. A huge sensation welled up in her, fury and disgust and misery, and she knew that she had to get away, get *away*, or the shaking would explode out of control. How *could* Soho do this to her?

'Angel!' Soho's voice went shrilly up the scale as Angel turned and ran. Someone made a grab for Angel; she glimpsed York's face and lashed out with her fingernails; he yelped in surprise and she was past him, racing towards the exit. Music dinned in her head, mixing with the sound of shouting voices. Twinkle wriggled on her shoulder and chirruped, 'I know a lovely little song—'

Angel gave an inarticulate yell, grabbed the Therapet and thrust it at someone – she didn't know who and didn't care – as she rushed past. Out of the exit, Soho still shouting but distant now; it sounded as if she was having hysterics. The glass walkway to the bubble-lift was ahead and Angel pounded along it, hoping against all hope that the lift would be there — *oh, please, let it be there waiting, don't let Soho and York catch up with me* — and it was there, and she jumped in and shouted, 'Down, I want to go down, I want to get *out* of here!'

The lift started to move. It seemed that no one had come after her, at least not yet, but just before the floor dropped out of sight Angel saw a little gold blur trotting clumsily but purposefully along the walkway, and heard a small voice calling, 'Angel! Come back, Angel! Please come back, Angel!' It was Twinkle, sounding so lonely and pitiful that Angel's conscience gave a huge, irrational stab before she reminded herself that the Therapet was only a computer device and not real.

As the lift gathered speed, whisking her away from the horrors of the party, she burst into tears.

When the lift disgorged her at the Experience Mart's exit level, Angel meant to take the safe, Vigilant-patrolled route to Gate Three, where she could pick up the String. But somehow she took a wrong turning, and when at last she managed to stop crying and calm the turmoil in her mind enough to take in her surroundings, she found herself instead in a long, echoing and eerily deserted gallery. There was a voice-guide panel on the wall, but it had been vandalised and was repeating, 'DEFECTIVE. DEFECTIVE' in a flat, dehumanised voice. The lighting was dim, there were no adstrips playing on the walls, and even the music had been turned off. Obviously, Angel thought, people didn't use this part of the Mart at night, and she shivered suddenly despite the heating. This was just the sort of area where marauders hung out . . .

Just as the thought crossed her mind she heard sounds in the distance; first a kind of irregular banging, then echoes that sounded like mad laughter, and a flurry of footsteps that cut off suddenly into silence. Angel's heart gave an unpleasant lurch. She thought the noises had come from somewhere to the right and, slipping off her shoes so that she could move quietly, she ducked into a side corridor and padded quickly along it. The corridor led to another gallery, better lit but still unnervingly quiet, and as she emerged into it Angel realised that it was the site of the art exhibition she had seen on her way to Interact a few days ago. She sighed with relief – this meant she was close to the Gate One String stop. There'd be Vigilants there and she would be safe, and she started to run past the art exhibits towards the exit at the far end.

She was halfway down the gallery when the marauders appeared. There were four of them, and they came through the exit ahead of her, kicking at the auto-aperture before it could fully open, so that it rang with a violent noise that seemed to echo through the entire Mart. Angel skidded to a halt, eyes widening in horror, and at the same moment the marauders saw her. They stopped. They stared. Then one of them, an incredibly thin, gangling boy of about eighteen with dead-white skin and blackened teeth, stepped forward. He was grinning, and he held something in his hand.

'Hey, what's this? On your own, sweetheart?'

Angel didn't answer but took a step back.

'She's shy,' one of the others said. 'Lost her Prime Parent

and doesn't know where to go-oh.'

'Yeah. But look at those clothes, and that face. Quite a wealthy little package.' The black-toothed one gave that horrible grin again. 'What's the matter, sweetheart? Synergymed amputate your tongue because you talked too much?'

A third marauder, a girl with no hair, who didn't look much older than Angel, sniggered. 'Why don't we take a look in her mouth and find out? Then if Synergymed haven't done their expensive job properly, we can finish it for them, nice and *cheap*!'

Angel knew she had only one chance. She braced her feet, braced the muscles in her legs, then spun round and bolted. She'd taken only four strides when there was a whining *zinggg* and something shot past her to explode on the floor in her path. With a scream she swerved as she realised that it was a stun–detonator – *but only the Vigilants were permitted to use those! Oh, Tokyo, if the marauders had got one they must have killed a Vigilant*—

'What's the rush, sweetheart?' a mocking voice called. 'The fun hasn't even *started* yet.'

She turned and saw Black–Teeth holding up the detonator-gun. One move, she realised, and he'd fire it again, and this time he probably wouldn't aim in front of her.

She took a step backwards. 'G-go away,' she quavered. 'Leave me alone, or I'll – I'll—'

'You'll what, rich girl? Shout for Prime Parent? Prime Parent's a lo-o-ong way away. There's just you, and us.'

'And soon,' added the hairless girl, 'there'll be just *us*.'

As their laughter and whistles rang through the gallery Angel stumbled backwards, and collided with something. Terrified, she spun round, but instead of coming face to face with another marauder she found herself looking at her own terrified self. Wildly a memory flashed through her mind; the mirrors-and-water sculpture called *Future Passed* – she'd seen a face in it before, a face she knew—

There was a rush of feet behind her and she screamed again, a panicking shriek as she tried to run and dodge and throw herself aside all at once. She lost her balance and one flailing hand made a frantic grab for the sculpture. The mirrors swung wildly, water cascaded over her arm, then suddenly she was falling . . .

Falling . . .

Falling into the middle of the sculpture, and . . .

. . . and *through* it . . .

There was a colossal flash of light. The thudding feet and whooping cries of the marauders swelled to an enormous crescendo, dinning in her ears – and a concussion of noise, brilliance and other, impossible things smashed through Angel's consciousness like an explosion.

FOUR

'*Ahh! O-o-o-o-o-oh!*'

The long-drawn scream came from Angel's own throat, but she didn't know it. All she did know was that she had slammed into an ice-cold wall that instantly opened and engulfed her. The freezing shock of it buffeted her brain; then suddenly she was through it, shooting upwards with a roaring din all around her, bursting out into brilliant light and hurtling forward—

She must have passed out for a few minutes, because the next thing she was aware of was lying face downwards on a surface that felt cold and raspy and horrible, soft on top but hard underneath the softness. There was a roaring, rushing sound somewhere behind her, an overpowering smell in her nostrils – and all her clothes were soaking wet.

Angel opened her eyes, and saw a greenish fuzz a centi from the end of her own nose. It was the source of the horrible smell, and with a new shock she realised what it was. Grass. She'd seen real grass at the Cultural Nostalgia Gardens, so she couldn't mistake it; in fact she'd programmed it into her Vee world of Avalonne, for a more authentic feel. But the Cultural Nostalgia grass wasn't like this. It was neat, clean, smooth, and it didn't smell of anything. This was horrible stuff; coarse and mucky and

41

squidgy. And there were things in it – things, she realised with a sudden inward jolt, that moved—

With a squeak of fright and revulsion, Angel jolted upright, shrinking away from the crawling things in the grass.

And jumped again, even more violently, as another voice echoed, '*Ahh!*'

Her head jerked up – and she came face to face with two women who were kneeling in the grass in front of her.

Angel's eyes opened wide with astonishment. Even in the extremes of her Vee inventions, she had never imagined any characters like these two. They had the strangest face-makes; plain and boring brown, with no decoration at all on their eyes or mouths or cheeks, and their hair looked as if it hadn't been cleansed or styled in even the smallest way, but had just been left to hang long and lank over their shoulders. As for their clothes . . . she'd never seen garments remotely like them: shapeless and baggy, the colours a sludgy, unco-ordinated motley in which everything merged drably with everything else. No one Angel knew, or had ever heard of, would have been seen dead looking the way they did.

Frozen moments seemed to pass while Angel stared at the women and the women stared back. They looked as shocked as she was, which was oddly comforting. Then, very tentatively, one of them reached out a hand towards her.

'Spirit Childe . . .' she said. 'You're awake!'

She was speaking the language that Angel spoke, but

her accent was like nothing Angel had ever heard before. And the words . . . *Spirit Childe*? Whatever was she *talking* about?

'Can you hear, Spirit Childe?' said the woman eagerly. 'Can you speak?'

Angel wasn't sure if she could do either any more, and even less sure that she wanted to try. Where the spiders *was* this place? Behind the two women her mind vaguely registered a blur of green ground and grey sky, but it meant nothing at all to her. She struggled to gather her memory together. One moment she'd been in the Experience Mart; then the marauders had appeared, she'd tried to run, and—

The sculpture. She'd fallen onto the sculpture. And now, *this*. What had *happened* to her?

The women were motionless, one still holding out her hand, both still staring. All three of them were like a frozen tableau, and suddenly logic came to Angel's rescue. She knew the answer to her question. This place and these people weren't real. They couldn't possibly be. So either she was dreaming, or she was in Vee and had got so engrossed in the fantasy world that it had temporarily taken over her mind. Well, there was an easy way to find out which, wasn't there?

Loudly and firmly Angel demanded: 'Programme terminate!'

She expected the world and the strange women to go away. But they did not. Instead, the women both flung their arms skyward and uttered whooping, ululating cries of delight.

'She speaks! She hears us!'

' "Programme Terminate" . . . what does it *mean*?'

'The Spirit Childe has her own mysterious ways! Perhaps she's giving us a riddle to solve?'

Angel's mouth worked dazedly, trying to protest, argue, ask a thousand questions, but no sound came. Then the woman who had held out her hand said, 'Fetch the others, quickly – we must make the Spiritual Circle and sing the welcome-chant for her!'

Her companion scrambled to her feet and sprinted away across the grass, towards what looked like a collection of brown heaps in the distance. She was yelling as she went, something about 'Over the stars' and 'Crystal Magick'. As her voice rang out shriekingly, other figures started to emerge from inside the heaps. People . . . lots more people . . . Slowly and horribly, it began to dawn on Angel that this was *not* a dream, and her gaze veered unsteadily back to the remaining woman. She was smiling now, a fixed, artificial smile, as though she was every bit as terrified as Angel felt. Angel swallowed something that was trying to block her throat, and her voice quavered out:

'Where *am* I?'

It was the corniest line from the corniest story-vid ever created, but it was the only thing she could say, because it was the thing she desperately wanted to know. The woman gasped as though Angel had just given her a priceless gift, and replied, 'O, Spirit Childe! You're with us now. You've come to us, and you will inspire us!'

Angel was completely confounded. As far as she knew she'd never inspired anyone in her life, and – certainly if

44

Cray was to be believed – she was never likely to. This was *insane*.

'Look,' she said, aware now that she was shivering on top of everything else, 'I don't know what you mean, and I don't know who you are, and I'm cold and I'm wet and this place is—'

She didn't finish, because from behind her came an extraordinary sound; part snort, part grunt, and part something that she couldn't begin to identify. And a breath of hot air blew on the back of her neck.

Angel spun round.

Angel Ravenhair of the Crystal Tower, Mistress of Sorcery, Lone Warrior of Light, knew all about horses. She had ridden her snow-white steed across the misty wastes of Vee-Avalonne more times than she could count, in pursuit of yet another valorous quest for love and/or justice. But Angel Ravenhair's steed and Angel Ashe's first encounter with a very large, very solid and utterly *real* horse were two thoroughly different matters altogether. The horse had lowered its head to her, so that its great, long face was only a few centis from her own. It flapped its lips, snorted again, and a belch of hot, reeking air engulfed Angel as it pushed its muzzle curiously towards her and sniffed her hair.

Angel did the only thing she was capable of doing in the wake of such a shock. She screamed, and then fainted.

She came back to consciousness to the sound of a chorus of singing voices. There was a sense of dimness around her, broken by occasional flickers of light that danced on the far side of her eyelids, and though a part of her wanted to open her eyes, the memory of the horse, coupled with a powerful and frantic desire to believe that this was *not* happening to her, made her screw them more tightly closed instead. The song carried on. The tune was a drone that sounded as fatuous as one of Twinkle's glitches, and the words seemed to be about such things as 'celestial sky' and 'crystal rain'. And one person was singing very, very flat.

Angel took a grip on herself and tried, very slowly and as calmly as she could manage, to *think*. She was lying down again, but on her back this time, with something scratchy but soft underneath her. She seemed to be wearing something equally scratchy . . . they must have taken her own clothes away; but at least whatever they had put her into was dry.

So, then. They'd given her dry clothes, and they were singing a song that — however infantile — at least sounded friendly. They hadn't killed her, and the horse hadn't eaten her (she'd created a man-eating horse in Avalonne, once, and the memory of it came back sharply and unpleasantly now). So far, so good. But the one vital question still hadn't been answered.

Where WAS she?

Angel opened her eyes.

The first things she saw were several unsteady pinpoints of light. Her vision was still unfocused and blurry, so she couldn't work out what they were, but they seemed to be the only source of illumination. Shadows gathered and closed in beyond them; she had the impression that she was surrounded by walls, but couldn't see far enough in the dimness to be sure.

Then she realised that some of the shadows were people. They stood in a circle around her, looking very solemn and singing their song with great concentration. They all had their arms outspread at their sides, and they were waving them slowly up and down, up and down. The whole spectacle looked so like one of Bright's pre-as dances that, under other circumstances, Angel wouldn't have been able to stop herself from laughing. As it was, though, she didn't laugh. Because this situation was *not* funny.

Then a new figure moved closer by, and someone leaned over her. The face swam into focus, and Angel saw a man with seamed, lined skin and long grey hair looking down at her.

'Are you all right, Spirit Childe?' He spoke with the same strange accent that the women had used. 'Have you recovered?'

Angel's throat was very dry, but she managed to croak, 'Wh-who are you . . .?'

He smiled beatifically. 'My name is Karma, and I am First Brother of our Village.'

Angel stared at him blankly, thinking: *Village? What the flackers is a Village?*

'You're not . . .' She coughed as her throat rasped. 'You're not marauders . . .?'

It was Karma's turn to look blank. 'Um . . . no,' he said, then the beatific smile returned. 'We are all Brothers and Sisters under the Sun and Moon, Children of the Stars,

Custodians of the Trees, Guardians of All Nature's Virtues!'
You could almost *hear* the capital letters in his speech,
Angel thought. Karma raised his arms and waved them
about in an incomprehensible gesture. 'And we welcome
the Spirit Childe, sent to us from Far Realms to bring
Love and Peace and Healing to All! Welcome, Spirit Childe
– welcome to Albion!'

The chorus behind him took up the chant. 'Welcome,
Spirit Childe! Welcome, Spirit Childe!' Angel bore it for
half a minute or so, then something within her snapped.

'Look.' She sat up abruptly, making Karma draw back
as if he was afraid they might accidentally make contact.
The song stopped again and she had the feeling that
everyone was listening intently. She looked, almost glared,
around at them. 'I don't know who you are, or what
happened to me, or where this Albion is, or anything else!
Will someone please *tell me what's going on*?'

Several people breathed 'Ah!', and Karma recovered his
courage and loomed again, clasping his hands before him.

'You have had a Long Journey, Spirit Childe,' he intoned.
'We shall give you Sustenance and Revivifying Magic to
help you!' Another set of enigmatic gestures, and he bowed.
'Tell us what you would like, and It Shall Be Given!'

Angel's throat was really hurting now; there was
something in the air here that irritated it beyond belief.
'I'd like a glitter-ice,' she said firmly. 'Silver Raindrops
flavour.' This never failed to refresh her.

Karma's face fell. 'Glitter . . . Ice?' he repeated.

'Yes. Silver Raindrops flavour.' Belatedly she
remembered her manners. 'Please.'

He seemed to understand then, and snapped out an order to someone in the shadows, who hastened away. Angel looked around. 'It's dark in here,' she said. 'Where's the house 'gig? Can't you tell it to bring the lights up?'

'Ah! I understand.' Karma beamed, and beckoned. Three people came forward. Each was carrying one of the pinpoints of light that Angel had seen earlier, and as they closed in, she frowned.

'Those aren't the only lights you have, surely?' Unthinkingly she reached out, touched one of the pinponts—

'*Oww!*' Her hand jerked away and she sucked her fingertip, then looked up at Karma in outraged shock. 'That's a real flame! It burned me!' Pain and anger swelled, and tears started in her eyes. 'What do you think you're *doing*, allowing these inside your apartments? Real fire's dangerous – it's anti-societal *and* Unpermitted!'

Karma was completely nonplussed by now, but was saved from replying by the return of the refreshment-fetcher, a girl a few years older than Angel. She was carrying what appeared to be a very crude drinking vessel; approaching, she shyly held it out, and Angel stopped sucking her burned finger for long enough to peer suspiciously inside.

Whatever was in the cup certainly wasn't glitter-ice. It looked, in fact, like plain water, and when she cautiously ventured to sip it, water was exactly what it proved to be. Angel pulled a face. Water was okay if you were desperate, she supposed, but this hadn't even been flavoured; it tasted of nothing whatsoever.

But it did ease her throat, so she drank it all and handed it back with a nod of thanks. Karma seemed pleased, and, drawing himself up as though preparing for a speech, began, 'And now, Spirit Childe—'

Confusion, her sore finger and the aftermath of shock were all conspiring to make Angel feel exhausted, and she didn't think she could cope with any more of Karma's capital letters at present. So before he got any further, she hastily interrupted him.

'Look . . . you said that whatever I wanted would be given. So . . . could you leave me alone? I want to sleep; just for a bit. I'll feel better for it, and then . . . well, maybe we can all talk and get this mess sorted out.'

Karma bowed and made more elaborate gestures. 'It shall Be as you Wish, Spirit Childe!' he declared, and turned to his hovering companions. 'The Spirit Childe will rest now! Out, all of you; out, out!'

They went, to Angel's enormous relief. Karma might have stayed and carried on talking, but she mustered a sweet smile and said pointedly. 'Goodbye.'

'Ah. Yes, of course. Goodbye, Spirit Childe.'

He left, through a peculiar-looking rectangle that opened on to more gloom and then shut again with a dull noise. Angel watched, holding her breath, until she was certain that he had truly gone, then turned to the control strip in her arm. Light, light . . . there must be some control on here that could tap into their house console. She tried code after code, and when all failed she tried swearing at the strip, but no matter what she did, nothing responded. Still the only illumination came from the real flames on

50

sticks, but after her first experience she was too afraid to look more closely at them and see if they could be adjusted.

At last she gave up her efforts and instead looked around to see what little could be seen in the semi-darkness. She appeared to be lying on a lumpy sack — there was no better word for it — made from something unimaginable, and covered with a very rough, fibrous material. Another sheet of the same material had been draped over her, and when she pushed it back (her entire body was itching ferociously now), she found that the dry garment she had been put into was equally bizarre. It looked as though someone had taken a sack, cut holes for head and arms and simply pulled it over her. No style, no design, and (as far as it was possible to tell) no colour co-ordination either. And it felt *awful*.

Depressed by the garment, she pulled the rough sheet up again and peered into the nether gloom. She was, as far as she could tell, in a room of sorts, though there were no familiar furnishings; in fact there seemed to be virtually no furnishings at all. There was no soft glow of a house console panel, so she concluded that the console must be elsewhere, but nonetheless she said aloud: 'Input: light control.'

No response; nothing lit up in any of the dark corners. Then a thought occurred to her and she tried another tactic. 'Input:' she said again. 'Network communications.' If she could just vid someone, find out where she was . . . but again, nothing happened, and Angel was forced to consider the unnerving possibility that this place did not even have normal computer facilities. That was so unlikely as to be almost unthinkable – yet what other conclusion could she draw?

Suddenly a wave of sheer misery washed over her. For a short while, and in a perverse way, she had almost been enjoying this situation. Barring the incident with the flame, it had been very much like an original and highly imaginative Vee adventure. But a Vee game could be halted whenever she chose. This could not; and she didn't understand what had happened to her, and no one here seemed able or willing to explain, and as the confusion of possibilities bubbled in her mind she was becoming more than a little frightened.

She huddled down under the rough covering, hugging herself. The room felt very cold, but she was all too well aware that the low temperature wasn't the only reason for the shivering that had begun to overtake her. Maybe, she thought desperately, maybe it really was a dream? Maybe she'd been hurt in the confrontation with the marauders in the Experience Mart, and though someone had rescued her she was now lying in a Synergymed cubicle, unconscious, in a coma even, while Soho wrung her hands at the cribside and medics strove to save her life . . .

Or maybe she hadn't been rescued. Maybe she was . . . *Dead*?

Angel's heart gave such a thump at that thought that she realised that it was nonsense and she was still (painfully) alive. But the coma-dream theory was a possibility. If she had—

Her train of exploration halted with a jerk as the

aperture on the far side of the room made its strange noise again.

She sat up, looked round, and saw that the aperture was opening. Karma? Why had he returned? She'd asked to be left alone; so what was he doing sneaking in, hoping to catch her asleep . . .?

Angel drew breath to call out a challenge. But the intruder beat her to it.

'Hello . . .?'

The voice was much younger than Karma's; nearer Angel's own age in fact. She felt herself relax fractionally, but her tone was still challenging as she demanded, 'Who's there?'

He didn't reply, but she heard footfalls on the floor, approaching. 'I asked for some peace and quiet,' she said testily. 'Karma said you'd all leave me alone.'

'I know. That's why I came.'

That got Angel's attention, and quickly she screwed her head round, her heart quickening again. There was a pale shape among the shadows; similar height and size to herself, she surmised, and wearing trousers instead of a long, baggy sack, but beyond that she couldn't make out any detail.

'Who are you?' she said.

He laughed. 'More to the point, who are *you*?'

She licked her lips. 'They keep calling me—'

'The Spirit Childe. Yes, I know. But you're not a Spirit Childe, are you? You're as ordinary and human as the rest of us. And I think I know where you came from.'

Angel froze. 'You *know* . . .?'

He started to move towards her again. 'I can't be sure, mind, but . . .' The shadows fell back then as he reached the little pool of light cast by the first flame-stick, and Angel saw him clearly for the first time.

He was a boy of about her own age, small, and slight almost to the point of thinness. His eyes were grey and his unkempt hair was completely white. But it was his face that shocked Angel, so much so that her heart almost stopped beating altogether — because she had seen it before.

It was the face she had first seen in the Experience Mart, frowning and muttering and looking back at her out of the mirror sculpture.

She whispered: 'Oh, Tokyo . . .'

The boy shook his head quizzically. 'Sorry, I don't understand; but then I probably wouldn't.' He came closer, sat down on the floor beside her, and extended a hand in a gesture that was quite new to Angel. 'Whoever you really are, welcome to Albion.' A tentative smile — and then he delivered the second shock, as he added, 'My name's Winter.'

FIVE

'All right now? Here, have some more of this. Are you sure you're all right?'

Angel nodded and took another mouthful of the water he had brought. The worst of it was wearing off and she felt better; it had simply been a case of temporary trauma, and the Peace pills that Soho had on regular order from SynergyMed could have dealt with it in a matter of seconds. But Soho wasn't here, and neither was SynergyMed or any of its pills, so she had just had to cope on her own.

With Winter's help.

The fact that the white-haired boy had the same name as her invented Vee-lover, coupled with the stunning familiarity of his face, struck Angel as little short of insane. It was little wonder that she had been incapable of doing anything but shiver and cry until, at last, Winter had managed to calm her down.

They were both now sitting on the stuffed bag that apparently passed for a crib here. Angel's face was still wet, but she didn't have any Cloudex to freshen her. Instead she sniffed, wiped her cheeks as best she could on the sleeve of the scratchy garment, and tried to marshal her thoughts.

'You said . . .' Another sniff. 'A few minutes ago, you

said, "Welcome to . . ." somewhere.'

'Albion,' Winter supplied.

Angel nodded. 'Right. So what and where is Albion?'

He lifted his shoulders. 'Our land. Here. Where we live.'

It was a far from satisfactory answer. Though Angel's geography was shaky at best, even she knew that there was nowhere called Albion in the Eurostates, or anywhere else that she had ever heard of. Besides, no location in her world was remotely like this. It *couldn't* be.

And that led to the alarming concept that she was no longer in her world at all.

Clasping and fidgeting her hands in front of her, she looked quickly, nervously at Winter again. 'You said something else. That you think you know where I came from.' A pause. 'Do you?'

Winter's expression grew cautious, but he said nothing. 'Please!' Angel urged him. 'I want to know. I need to!'

He hesitated, debating with himself, then abruptly let his breath out in a rapid rush. 'Listen,' he said. 'If I tell you what I really think, will you promise on the full moon not to say a word to any of the others?'

Angel wasn't about to be manoeuvred into a corner, so she demanded, 'Why?'

'Because it wouldn't fit in with what *they* believe happened.' Winter's grey eyes took on a flinty edge. 'And that would make life a lot more complicated for us both.'

What was he implying? Angel couldn't be sure, but she didn't entirely like the sound of it.

'Well?' Winter asked after a few moments' silence. 'Do you promise?'

If she wanted to find out any more, she didn't have a lot of options. Angel nodded curtly. 'Yes.'

He seemed relieved. 'All right: then I'll tell you what I know — or what I've guessed, anyway. When you appeared through the waterfall—'

'When I *what*?'

Winter blinked. 'You don't remember?'

'No, I do *not* remember!' Angel said furiously. 'One moment I was in the Experience Mart, and there were — oh, never mind!' He wouldn't comprehend; she could see that in his face. 'I haven't the *least* idea of how I appeared here! I kept asking that man — Korma, or whatever his name is — but he was too busy gushing his spidering Spirit Childe garbage to give me any answers!' She took several deep breaths to bring her temper back under control, then added, 'I think I'd like you to tell me, Winter. Right now.'

So Winter explained. And the story was as baffling to Angel as everything else that had happened to her.

A group of Winter's people had apparently been holding some sort of celebration outside on the grass. The idea of anyone in their right mind having a party in the unhealthy and hazardous outdoors boggled Angel, but she bit back the comments she might have made and listened. There was, Winter said, a cliff face nearby, overhung with trees and with a waterfall cascading down it to a pool that fed a stream. The group had all been chanting (Angel didn't ask what or why) and were gathered in a semicircle before the rocks when at the heart of the waterfall there was a sudden peculiar flicker of light. It flared outwards, flickered again, vanished — and Angel fell out of the cascade as

57

though someone had violently thrown her. She pitched straight into the pool; as she surfaced again the group hauled her out, and . . . 'Well, you know the rest,' Winter finished.

'You mean that I actually came *through* the waterfall?' Angel said incredulously.

Winter nodded. 'Out of nowhere. I was there: I saw it.'

Nothing can come literally out of nowhere, Angel told herself; *that's against all the laws of physics.* 'What's behind the waterfall?' she asked.

Winter's face became wary. 'Behind it . . .?'

'That's what I said. Behind the water. What's there?'

He shrugged. 'Nothing much. Rocks and things.'

His attitude was enough to tell her that he was not telling the entire truth, and she leaned forward, grasping hold of his wrist with a strength that clearly surprised him. 'Winter,' she said, 'you're hiding something, and if you don't tell me what it is, then I'll—'

She stopped. That noise again – the aperture at the far end of the room was opening—

'Winter!' Karma, holding a light-stick, spoke sternly from the threshold. 'Who gave you permission to come here disturbing the Spirit Childe?'

Winter had scrambled to his feet, his posture defensive and his expression mingling guilt and alarm. 'I'm sorry, Karma,' he floundered. 'I just – I mean, I thought—'

Angel's brain moved fast, almost without any conscious direction. 'I called out,' she said quickly, wondering at the same time what instinct had urged her to protect Winter.

'I called, and he heard me and came to see if I was all right.'

She couldn't tell whether Karma was convinced by the lie, for he made no comment but only walked towards them. Stopping a few steps away he glowered at Winter and said, 'Out.'

As Winter left, Angel saw the mute look of appeal he flung at her, and she nodded fractionally to let him know that she would keep her promise and say nothing. The aperture swung shut behind him (it really was an extraordinary contraption, she thought) and Karma cleared his throat.

'Spirit Childe, are you rested?'

Angel was tempted to retort that chance would have been a fine thing and she thought she had asked for some peace and quiet. But she resisted the temptation. There were a good many more facts that she wanted to find out, and she would learn more by being pleasant.

So she said, 'Yes, thanks. And I want to know a few things. Quite a lot of things, in fact.'

Karma made a bow, as he had done before. 'Whatever you wish, of course,' he said deferentially. 'The Spirit Childe is Sent Among Us, and All that is Ours is Hers!' He smiled. 'Ask, Spirit Childe. Ask, and We Shall Answer. But first—' He clapped his hands, and to Angel's chagrin the aperture smacked back again and a whole gaggle of people came in. They must have been lurking outside, waiting for the summons. And with an awful, sinking certainty she knew they were going to start singing again.

Oh, well. If they must perform their rituals . . . What

would Angel Ravenhair of the Crystal Tower have done? She would have put up with it, Angel decided. Indulged them. So perhaps it would stand her in good stead to be Angel Ravenhair for a while; until they had finished their game and could be persuaded to talk some sense. Besides, it might be wiser not to say too much until she had the chance to speak to Winter again, alone.

She returned Karma's smile, and resigned herself to being Welcomed Among His People.

Angel's first night in Albion was not a good one.

The building (for want of a better word) that she was in turned out to be the home not only of Karma but of nearly a dozen other adults, too. They all seemed to be Paired to each other, which was extremely confusing, and she had the impression that they were the most important people in the community and, fundamentally, ran everything. She gathered that it was a great privilege to be housed under their roof, but she found it hard to believe that these unspeakably primitive surroundings were the best that they could do for a supposedly honoured guest.

So far, she had only once left the room in which she had woken up. When she had asked where the bathing and privacy cubicles were, what they had shown her was horrifying. No air-shower or whirlpool, not even an ancient-style bath (baths were fashionable in Zone Bohemia at the moment; there was a Retro craze in furnishings). There was just a dark, reeking space, containing a bench made of actual wood with a round hole in it that led down to some unimaginable nether region. When Angel realised what she was expected to use this for, she nearly had a hysterical fit. But this, it seemed, was quite normal to the Albionites. There *was* nothing else, and it was a case of suffer it or flit – as Soho would have said – to a better Zone. Angel suffered it, just. But afterwards she felt so nauseated that she had to lie down again.

The Albionites didn't understand her reaction, but they were very kind and solicitous. However, their idea of kindness was to gather round her and sing yet another song, after which they plied her with food that looked and smelled appalling, and which doubtless would also have tasted appalling if she had had the courage to try it. Angel was hungry, but she firmly refused everything they offered her, and at last they all went away. Though she had no way of telling the time, she had the feeling that it was quite late into the night when she was finally left alone, and she settled as best she could on the stuffed bag, pulling the cover over herself. She didn't want to sleep. There was far too much to think about, and as she lay in the darkness her mind churned over all that had happened, and tried to make sense of what little she had been able to discover.

She had asked Karma where Albion was, but his answer had been as vague as Winter's. Angel had the distinct impression that these people didn't know much about any places beyond their own boundaries; or, if they did, they didn't care. She had then tried asking about dates and years, to see if that gave her any clues. But the Albionites' calendar was incomprehensible: this, apparently, was the Fourth Moon in the Year of the Fallow Deer, which to

Angel meant a resounding zero.

She had given up trying to get her bearings at that point, and questioned Karma instead about her own arrival here. He confirmed what Winter had already told her: that she had appeared out of the waterfall that cascaded into what Karma called the 'Pool of Spiritual Communion'. Whatever the name meant, it was obviously an important place, and it tied in somehow with the Albionites' notion of Angel as some kind of magical visitor – the 'Spirit Childe' – who would bring them good fortune. It was on the tip of Angel's tongue to protest that there was nothing spiritual or magical about her, she was just an ordinary human being. But at the last moment she had decided that it might, after all, be better to let them go on deluding themselves. As a Spirit Childe, she was being treated like a VIP – if her hosts found out the real truth, they might not be quite so kind and generous. The promise she had made to Winter (and kept) raised her suspicions just a fraction; if he was so anxious to keep his own theories a secret, then he must surely have a reason? Until she found out what that reason was, Angel concluded that it would be wiser to keep smiling, play the role the Albionites had assigned to her, and say as little as possible about anything.

Finally, she fell asleep. When she woke, a grey smear of daylight was showing through the window. And when necessity got the better of squeamishness and she steeled herself to face the reeking cubicle, she found Winter waiting for her.

He put a finger to his lips, warning her to silence, and

beckoned her towards the house's main aperture (properly, she'd discovered, called a door). Angel pointed to the cubicle; he nodded and mimed that he would meet her outside.

When she emerged (she was getting the hang of using the doors now), she stopped dead on the threshold. The sun was just rising in a clear blue sky, and the entire scene before her was steeped in a pale, cool light that made the world look newly made. Angel stared and stared; in the closed, sheltered and synthetic surroundings of her own world she had never seen anything to compare with this.

The Village was situated in a long, broad valley that sloped gently downwards towards the sunrise. The landscape was a tapestry of subtle greens and golds and browns; open grassy meadows rising on either side in steepening slopes where trees — *real* trees — grew thickly, flourishing upwards and outwards in a froth of dense foliage. Closer by, there were more trees, smaller and lower and studded with white blossom, and little plants grew in neat rows between them. Pivoting slowly, Angel saw the Village itself; a collection of long, low buildings with stone or wood walls and straw roofs; and beyond them, where the valley narrowed and began to climb, were high rock walls and, half-hidden among all the vegetation, the glitter of water. The scene looked like something out of Avalonne, and she sighed with the sheer delight of it.

'It's . . . *beautiful!*' she said.

Winter nodded but he didn't make any comment, saying instead, 'I thought we ought to talk. Before Karma and the others wake up. Come on. We'll go to the waterfall.'

He led her past the cluster of the Village and into the narrowing funnel of the valley. Leaving the buildings behind, they started to climb an uphill, zigzagging path. It was very uneven (Angel kept stumbling, until Winter held on to her arm to steady her), and it seemed to go on for light-years, until her legs ached blazingly. She might have protested, but firstly she didn't have enough breath for it, and secondly – more importantly – she was very, very eager to see the waterfall, and hear what Winter had to say.

At last they plodded round a curve in the track, and came to a place where the valley opened and levelled out to a rough, grassy bowl, fringed with bushes. Behind the bushes a rock face rose sharply. At the foot of the cliff was a pool, from which a stream flowed, chuckling away through a narrow cleft. And at the back of the pool was the waterfall.

Angel stopped, staring at the fall, and her first overwhelming feeling was one of disappointment. She had expected a magnificent, glittering cataract, shimmering with rainbow colours as it plunged down from a dramatic and dizzying height. This was nothing of the sort. It was just a straightforward stream of water, not much wider than she was, and the combination of dull daylight and the moss and weed growing on the rocks gave it a grey and rather grubby look.

She said: 'Oh.'

Winter heard the disillusion in her voice and smiled wryly. 'Not exactly a Spirit Childe sort of thing, is it?' he said. 'But it's where you came from.'

Remembering what had happened after her arrival, she licked her lips uneasily. 'Where's that horse?' she asked.

'Old Acorn? Around somewhere, I expect. Probably grazing over on the other side of the valley.' Winter's eyebrows went up quizzically. 'You're not scared of him, are you?'

'No, of course not,' Angel said quickly and firmly. She gazed at the water again. The pool at the foot of the fall looked deep and cold; very unpleasant, in fact. If the villagers hadn't been here to pull her out . . .

But they had been here, and she hadn't drowned, and now she was in this weird world and there were a great many questions to which she wanted answers.

Turning to face Winter, she said, 'Last night, you said you've got a theory about where I came from, but it doesn't fit in with what the others think.'

'Yes,' said Winter.

'And it's something to do with the waterfall, isn't it?'

A pause. Then: 'Yes.'

'Right.' Angel moved to the edge of the pool and narrowed her eyes at the cascade. 'When I asked you what's behind the waterfall, you said it was just rocks and so forth. I don't believe you. So I think you'd better tell me the truth.'

The second pause was far longer than the first. Angel could almost feel Winter debating with himself, and she knew instinctively that he was trying to decide whether or not he could trust her. Words wouldn't convince him – he didn't yet know her well enough – so she stayed silent, trying to be patient, until at last he spoke.

'All right,' he said, and let his breath out as though he'd been holding it for some time. 'It'd be better to show you, but I daren't do that now; the others will be awake soon and some of them might come up here.' He came to join her at the edge of the pool. 'Truth is, I don't *know* what's behind the fall. I mean, I've *seen* it, but I've no idea what it is.'

'Seen it? You mean, you went through the water and looked?'

He nodded. 'There's a cave near the bottom of the cliff face. You can't see it from this side because of the water, and I'm fairly sure no one else knows it's there. And there's something in the cave. A sort of . . . contraption.'

'What does it look like?'

Winter spread his hands helplessly. 'It doesn't look like anything I've ever seen before. It's sort of oblong, but with all different shapes inside it; and parts of it reflect things.'

Angel's pulse began to speed up. 'Reflect . . .?'

'Yes. The way water does when the sun's on it.' He frowned. 'I saw my own face in it, only it was much clearer than a water reflection. And when I touched it, it felt cold and smooth and very hard.'

A mirror . . . Angel thought. 'So,' she said carefully, 'what do you think it has to do with me?'

His throat moved as he swallowed. 'You're not going to believe me,' he said.

'Try me.'

'Well . . . I've been back to look at it several times since I first found it, trying to work out what it could be for and who could have put it there. One of those times, I was looking at the shiny surface, and instead of seeing my reflection, I saw . . . someone else's.'

Her pulse was really racing now. 'Whose, Winter? Whose face?'

He looked at her, and the hint of despair in his eyes gave the game away before he answered. 'Yours,' he said.

The art exhibition, the mirror sculpture, the face that she herself had seen staring and muttering in the glass-and-water reflections . . . 'Oh, Tokyo!' Angel whispered. 'Then it *was* you!'

The barriers of doubt and distrust collapsed, and she told Winter her story. Or, at least, as much of it as he could understand, because after a minute or two it became obvious that he was completely baffled by the idea of life in Eurostate-8. Everyday things like Schol, the String, Vid/Vee communication, were completely alien concepts to him, and the more Angel tried to explain, the more confused he became. At length she gave up, and cut her tale down to the bare bones. The sculpture (he did, at least, understand the notion of art), the fact that she had seen his face in the mirrors, and the marauders' assault that had led to her falling into the middle of the exhibit, to emerge with a scream out of the waterfall in Albion.

When she had finished, Winter said nothing for quite a while. He was frowning, and beneath the frown's mask she could see that he was struggling to get to grips with something momentous. Then, suddenly and unexpectedly, he reached out, put an arm around her shoulders and squeezed her in an awkward sort of way.

'You know, don't you,' he said, 'that you're not in your world any more?'

Angel was astonished. None of her friends at home ever hugged each other; only parents made affectionate gestures, and even then – certainly if Soho was an example – not very often. Angel's heart caught with a wistful little lurch, and for no logical reason she felt tears starting to her eyes. Blinking them away, she laughed with a catch in her voice.

'Don't look so worried. I'd worked that out, and I'm not going to start having a Syndrome about it.' Feeling uncomfortable suddenly, she stepped away from him. 'The trouble is, I don't know where your world – this world – is. It might be on another planet. It might be—'

'—in another time,' Winter interrupted. Angel's eyes widened, and he continued. 'Think about it. That sculpture – you said it was called "Future Passed", didn't you? So what does that suggest? The future, and the past.' He paused. 'I've always believed it was possible to travel in time, if only we could find out how to do it. I think you *have* done it. I think you've gone through a time-door, and you've come back hundreds of years into the past. And those shining surfaces – the mirrors, you called them – I think they're the key.'

SIX

Angel didn't want to go back to the Village. Her one thought was to explore behind the waterfall and see the object Winter described for herself. She was convinced it would be a match with the exhibit in the Experience Mart, and she was desperate to test out its properties and see if the doorway could be opened again. But Winter said no. Time was against them, he argued: the rest of the Village would be awake by now, and it was vital that they shouldn't be discovered up here together. Nothing she said or did would change his mind, so at last she had no choice but to give way.

'But what's the problem?' she protested as, reluctantly, she set off with him back down the track. 'For Tokyo's sake, all we've got to say is that you brought me to see the pool, and we had a splash in it!'

Winter shook his head vigorously. 'If Karma knew I'd taken you to the Pool of Spiritual Communion, he'd jump over the stars with fury.'

'Why?'

'Because it isn't my place to take you there. He's the First Brother, and I'm nobody.' Winter shrugged. 'He doesn't like me anyway. It's mutual, so I don't care much. But he'd bark at the moon if he caught me getting too friendly with the Spirit Childe.' He hurried on another

69

few paces, then added, 'And if he got wind of that thing behind the waterfall, and connected it with you, there'd *really* be trouble.'

'Now, look!' Angel stopped in the middle of the track and put her fists on her hips. 'What *is* all this story-vid about Karma? What does he actually think I am?'

Winter looked back at her, blankly. 'A Spirit Childe,' he said.

'And what *is* that, for Tokyo's sake?'

'You don't know?' His face was a study in astonishment, and Angel felt her patience ebbing.

'No,' she said ferociously, 'I do *not* know, because no one's bothered to *tell* me! It's obviously something special, or your people wouldn't be doing hyper-turns about me all over the place. But that's all I've worked out, because we don't have Spirit Children where I come from!'

He still looked baffled, but struggled to find an answer. 'Well . . . a Spirit Childe is . . . a being from another world.'

'Right. So far, it fits, doesn't it?'

'No, it doesn't. A Spirit Childe has special powers.'

'What sort of powers?'

'Oh . . . the usual things. Making prophecies. Curing illness. Generally performing miracles.' He shrugged. 'Karma doesn't think you're human. He thinks you were specially sent to us from the world of spirits; like a – a –' He groped for a word that she might understand. 'Like a sort of goddess.'

Angel knew about gods and goddesses. She'd come across the idea of them in mythology-vids, and had created several theoretical ones in Avalonne, though they

70

were only vague concepts and never actually put in an appearance. But they didn't really *exist*. Everyone knew that. And as for the idea of being one herself . . .

She sighed exasperatedly. 'This is crazy! Whatever Karma does or doesn't think I am, you know that I'm just a human being like you. So why don't we tell him the truth?'

'That,' said Winter, 'would be a very big mistake.'

'Why? All right, I know Karma's a bit of a spider, but he means well.' She frowned. 'Doesn't he?'

'Of course he does. As long as everything's going the way he wants it to. While he thinks you're a Spirit Childe, he'll carry on treating you as special. But if he finds out you're not, his attitude's going to change.'

'To what?' Angel asked.

Winter opened his mouth to answer, but before he could, a high, ululating call echoed across the valley from the direction of the Village.

'Oh, withering grass!' he said urgently. 'That's Charm, calling the goats for milking – we'd better run, or someone'll find out that we're not where we should be!'

He started to pound on down the track. Angel shouted, 'Winter, wait! You haven't finished explaining!' but he shouted back, 'No time now! We'll try to talk later, when there's no one around!' He paused. 'And not a word to *anyone*! Believe me, it's safer!'

She wanted to go after him, grab him, stop him and make him tell her so much more. But her feet were killing her – gold–and–silver softwire sandals were far from ideal footwear around here; hers were already falling apart, which put running right out of the question. Besides, he was already too far ahead. Calling him a complete frog under her breath, Angel stumbled achingly on towards the Village.

Winter was out of sight by the time she reached the first buildings. But other people were about, and at the sight of her a cry went up.

'Spirit Childe, Spirit Childe!'

'Oh, isn't she beautiful?'

'Over the stars!'

'Let's welcome her, sing to her!'

They came running, gathering round Angel like a drone of fans round a celebrity, and with demented, arm–waving gestures they started up yet another of their interminable chants. Angel put on a helpless, artificial smile and waved her own arms vaguely around in response, which brought a chorus of delighted wails. Then abruptly and deferentially a section of the crowd parted, and Karma appeared.

'Ah, Spirit Childe!' He made one of his elaborate bows, beaming like the rising sun. 'Welcome, Welcome, and thrice Welcome to this Wondrous Morning! And now, if you will Consent to Step into my Humble Dwelling, we shall Sustain you with the Best of All Good Things from our Table!'

It took Angel a moment or two to realise that he was talking about breakfast. Or Breakfast, as he would doubtless have put it. Her heart sank at the thought and she looked around for Winter, but he was nowhere in sight. All she could do was resign herself to the inevitable.

Still smiling her false smile, though more desperately

than ever, Angel Consented to follow Karma to his Humble Dwelling, to face what passed for food in Albion.

Angel didn't get a chance to talk to Winter again that day. She glimpsed him around the Village from time to time, but could never manage to contrive a direct meeting without at least one other person being in earshot. By the time evening came she was tying herself in knots with frustration, but there was nothing she could do.

It had been quite a day. In the afternoon, the Albionites had performed another welcoming ritual for their Spirit Childe. It was held out of doors, and like yesterday's antics it consisted of a lot of chanting and gesturing, though spiced up this time with a disorganised dance in which everyone joined, waving scarves and garlands around like streamers and stopping every so often to whoop loudly before running and hugging the nearest tree. They hugged a lot of things, Angel noticed – trees, bushes, animals, each other – and they also seemed to like rolling around on the ground. She asked Karma what it all meant, and he waffled at great length about 'Getting in Touch with our Spiritual Selves'. She nodded as if she understood, and said 'Oh', and 'Of course' and pretended that it all made sense.

When the sun set (disappointingly, there was no magnificent gold and crimson display in the sky; it simply got dark) everyone went indoors. This, she was told, was the Ninth Night of the Waxing Moon, which was apparently the time for Astrological Divination. Angel had no idea what Astrological Divination was, and Karma's efforts to explain left her none the wiser. But at least she wasn't expected to join in, so she thankfully escaped to her room for some peace and quiet.

She hoped that Winter might come looking for her, but he didn't. From another part of the Dwelling she could hear a distant drone of voices as the Divination progressed, and she guessed that Winter was there with the others and couldn't get away. Never mind. She'd get up early tomorrow, and find him before anyone else was around.

Angel slept a good deal better than on her first night in Albion, apart from some disquieting dreams about Soho, which woke her several times through the dark hours. The dreams brought a guilty pang. Since arriving here she had hardly spared a thought for Soho or Kim or anyone else in her own world, but she suddenly realised that they must be desperately worried about her. Had they called in the Vigilants? Was a huge search under way? How much must it all be costing?

And, above all, how was she ever going to find her way back?

By the time dawn broke, she couldn't wait any longer to see Winter. Listening carefully, she heard no sounds of anyone else up and about, so she tiptoed to the door, opened it and peered out.

This Dwelling, as Karma called it, was by far the largest building in the Village. It was a veritable warren of different rooms leading off one another or linked by poky passages; Angel surmised that it would take her a year at the very least to get to know it all and find her way around with any confidence. Karma, and the dozen other important people, had rooms in the inner section: Then in the outer rooms were several people of around Angel's age, who seemed to have no Prime Parent but were loosely 'looked after' by Karma and the other Big Noises. Winter was among their number, but Angel didn't know which room was his. Oh, well . . . she would just have to find it by a process of trial and error.

She ventured along the narrow passage. It was almost pitch dark – the only light was a dull grey drizzle from a window somewhere at the far end – but no way would Angel have trusted a light-stick, even if she had known how to set fire to one. For several minutes she groped her way along, turning corners, walking into walls that she couldn't see until they loomed from the gloom a finger's width from her face; after the third collision, she realised that this was hopeless. Winter's room could be anywhere: if she carried on like this, she was as likely as not to walk slap through Karma's door, and that would be the end of her plan.

She managed, at last, to find her way outside. The sunrise was as unspectacular as last night's sunset, and it was raining. Angel stood under the Dwelling's grass-roofed porch, staring around at the dismal morning and wondering what to do next. Then, to her left, a voice said, 'Oh! Spirit Childe . . . may I be of service to you?'

It was one of the women she had first encountered on her arrival. Angel thought her name was Sky but couldn't be sure. She was standing with hands clasped deferentially and an awed, expectant look on her face that made Angel feel embarrassed.

'Ah . . .' Angel got out. 'I was — that is, I — was looking for Winter.'

Sky looked surprised and a little disappointed. 'Winter?' she echoed.

'Yes.' Angel smiled at her. They all seemed to like it when she smiled at them. 'Can you tell me where he is, please?'

'He isn't here, Spirit Childe,' Sky replied. 'He's gone.'

'*Gone*?' Angel was appalled, but quickly masked it, recovering her composure. 'Where?'

'To the Plain of Silver Crystals, by the Shore of Ever-Changing Tides.'

'The *what*?' Angel demanded, completely bemused.

Sky beamed hopefully. 'We go there to gather and purify the crystals, and to harvest the tide's living bounty to nurture our land,' she said. 'This time it's Winter's turn to be one of the harvesters. The cart left last night — the stars showed us through our divinations that it was the right time to go.'

Angel knew nothing whatever about salt marshes or seaweed fertiliser, and her only experience of the sea was through Vee holidays or Avalonne programmes. But it was obvious that Winter had been sent off somewhere to do something that the Villagers considered important.

'Oh, flackers!' she said. 'When will he be back?'

Sky spread her hands vaguely. 'If the stars and the spirits are with them, they will return in three days — but it could be four, or even five.' Then her expression brightened. 'Though with your blessing, Spirit Childe, we know that the harvest will be bountiful!'

'Right,' said Angel. 'Yes. I see.' She didn't, really. But the fact remained that Winter had been sent away from the Village and would be uncontactable for quite some time. Was it a deliberate move on Karma's part, to separate them? No; surely not. Karma didn't know about their discussions, so he could have no possible reason for being suspicious. It was simply a piece of bad luck.

'Right,' she said again; then, seeing that Sky was waiting eagerly for some more significant response, she waved her arms in her general direction and smiled again. 'Thank you very much.'

She left Sky exulting over her encounter with the Spirit Childe, and went back inside the Dwelling feeling thoroughly frustrated.

With no other option to choose from, Angel resigned herself to waiting patiently for Winter's return. Her only compensation was the fact that there was so much to absorb, and so many demands on her time, that being patient wasn't too difficult. And at least she could learn more about Albion by her own methods.

Shock, she decided after a couple more days, was a very unpredictable thing. Faced with her present situation it would be perfectly logical for any normal person to have gone straight into a hyper-neuro episode, complete with paroxysms and hysteria syndrome, which would take months of medication and Societal Adjustment counselling to cure. But the anticipated reaction hadn't happened: in fact, now that the first overwhelming reaction was over, she was remarkably calm and clear-headed. She was even beginning to *enjoy* this adventure; for it had more than a little in common with her Vee-world of Avalonne. Green countryside, blue skies (well, grey more often than not; but she often programmed bad weather into Avalonne, so that was in keeping, too), rustling trees and chuckling streams . . . the two worlds were strikingly similar. And there were definite advantages over life in Zone Bohemia. No Soho, no Cray, no threat of First Pairing with an earwig like Bright. For the first time ever outside of Vee, Angel felt alive. She could almost *like* it here.

However, Albion did take some getting used to. To begin with, Angel had found it hard to handle the fact that she could not get food, light, temperature control or anything else she wanted by simply summoning a 'gig or using the control-strip implant in her arm. She knew that in ancient times computers had not existed, but accepting it in reality took a lot of practice. Albion was breathtakingly primitive and (she thought at first) breathtakingly dangerous – the people relied on real fire for almost everything. The light-sticks (which, she discovered, were called 'candles', with larger and even more frightening versions known as 'lamps'), were the only source of illumination, and for both warmth and the making of food they set fire to wood and turf and actually let it burn without any protection or even evaporators standing by. How it was that houses and people weren't incinerated on a daily basis, Angel didn't know. But as time passed and there were no catastrophes, her fear of fire began to wane.

She was also growing used to the awful materials that

were used for clothes, drapes, crib-covers and everything else that required fabric in some shape or form. At first their coarseness had brought her out in a hideous rash, but one of the women in the Village had given her a salve to put on her skin, and to her surprise it had worked fairly well.

The food was harder to adjust to – it tasted unutterably disgusting; the flavours were so powerful, and the textures so hard or chewy or fibrous, that Angel thought she would never be able to digest it. She would much rather have gone without; but her appetite was the same in this world as it had been in Eurostate 8, so at last she admitted defeat and forced herself to eat the vile diet. The drinking water was better, but tasteless, so on the second evening of Winter's absence she tried something called 'beer' that the Villagers made by a complicated process using different plants. She drank one cup – and the result was terrifying; for a whole evening she swayed and staggered, unable to keep her balance, while the world seemed to spin around her. Eventually she was violently sick, then she fell asleep and woke in the morning with a pounding headache that didn't ease until the day was half over. In her world, a drink that did that to you would be completely Unpermitted, and Angel resolved to leave beer well alone.

Then there were the animals. The Albionites kept a lot of animals, all of them alarmingly real. The horse that had terrified her almost out of her mind on her arrival was called Acorn, and was apparently used to pull a cart (the peasants she had programmed into Avalonne had carts, so she knew all about them). Acorn and the cart were now at the Shore of Ever-Changing Tides, wherever and whatever that was, but the Villagers had two other, smaller ponies, and they were much less daunting. Angel Ravenhair rode a snow-white steed, after all – though there were differences: horses in Avalonne didn't smell, bite or defecate, and they didn't have minds of their own. Horses in Avalonne always did exactly what you wanted them to. But for all their faults, real horses were fascinating; and by slow degrees she was also losing her squeamishness about the goats, pigs, chickens and other assorted creatures that the Albionites seemed to keep as pets. (No one explained their real purpose to her. They thought it too earthy for a Spirit Childe's sensitivities, which was probably just as well.)

The people of the Village were still being as kind as ever to Angel, and she was becoming accustomed to the daily rituals that they still performed in her honour. Their entire lives, she had noticed, were steeped in ritual; quite why they did it was still something of a mystery, but she had the impression that it was something to do with Religion. This struck her as deeply weird: at home, Religion was only believed in by a few cranky cultists; though she did vaguely recall from history-vids that centuries ago it had been very important, so perhaps that explained it. Whatever the case, the Albionites were completely wrapped up in it. They chanted to the sun in the mornings, to the moon at night, and to the trees or bushes or grass whenever they felt like it. They sang songs and danced dances; they piled up heaps of stones and gathered round them to make incomprehensible speeches about things like 'Earth Power' and 'Shining Vision' and 'Radiant Joy'. It was crazier than the Nature's Kisses vid-ads. But they seemed happy, and they continued to treat Angel as Someone Special – and she in her turn played up to the Spirit Childe role they had created for her.

Four days passed, and still Winter had not returned. Then, on the fifth day, came the first hint of trouble.

Angel was in her room. It was mid-afternoon, raining again, and she was feeling tired and out of sorts and a little grumpy. She had dreamed about Soho again last night, and her conscience was plaguing her. It wasn't that she particularly wanted to go back to Zone Bohemia, not now; she liked the freedom of Albion, and liked its similarities to Avalonne. She liked the fact that here she was looked on as an independent person with feelings of her own, rather than just as a nuisance to be tolerated. But her mother *must* be worried. Surely she must? And that brought back the pangs of guilt.

She was slouched on the crib feeling sorry for herself when the door opened and Karma appeared.

'Spirit Childe!' He hurried towards her, and she saw that he was highly agitated. 'Spirit Childe, we are in Need of your Help and Guidance!'

'Mine?' Angel said in alarm, sitting up straight. 'Why? I mean, how?'

Karma clasped his hands together. Everyone but Winter did that when they talked to her, she had noticed. 'We are Blighted!' he announced with great drama. 'The Powers of Earth and Water have seen fit to Turn Their

Hand Against Us, and the Sky Cries Ruin Upon Our Crops.'

Angel thought she grasped his meaning. 'Well, it has been raining a lot . . .' she said.

'Indeed; indeed.' Karma nodded dolefully and, to her relief, lapsed into something like comprehensible speech. 'It's the Potatoes, Spirit Childe. The plants are still young, but the Rain has Blighted them with Mildew.'

'Ah . . .' Potatoes? Mildew? Oh, spiders, whatever were *they*? Angel licked her lips uneasily. 'And you want me to . . . help?' she hazarded.

Karma's gloom lifted. Eagerly he agreed that that was exactly what they wanted. She got the gist of it, eventually: it seemed that some of the foodstuff plants they grew were going soggy and useless because of the rain, and unless there was a bit of sunshine pretty soon, the whole crop would be lost, and everyone would go hungry.

Then Karma delivered the body-blow.

'In Seasons Past,' he said, 'we have Bowed to the Will of the Earth Powers and Accepted our Sad Loss. But now . . .' He raised his arms as though welcoming the much-needed sun. '*Now*, we know that You Will Save Us!'

Angel goggled at him. 'Me . . .?' she repeated in a tiny voice.

'But of course.' Karma bowed, beamed, bowed again. 'After all, dear Spirit Childe, it is the Reason Why You Were Sent To Us.'

Horrified, Angel began, 'But I wasn't—' and then hastily bit the protest back. Karma was holding out his hands to her now, bowing a third time, inviting her to get up.

'Come, Spirit Childe,' he said. 'All has been Made Ready. Come, and Use Your Magic to Bring Back the Sun!'

SEVEN

Every single person in the Village was waiting for Angel when Karma led her outside. At the sight of their smiling, expectant faces, Angel felt a lurch of sheer panic, and the real meaning of Winter's warning came home to her with a slam. The Albionites were being so nice to her because they thought she had Special Powers – and now the time had come for her to prove it.

She couldn't control the weather, of course! In Avalonne, it would have been easy; she had programmed several disasters into her adventures there, and Angel Ravenhair had cured them (after a great and heroic struggle) with magic. But this wasn't Avalonne, and she wasn't Angel Ravenhair; not here, not any more. This was all too horribly *real*.

· The rain drizzled down on her head as, hoping that her quivering legs wouldn't give way under her, she unwillingly trailed in Karma's wake to where a tall, rickety 'throne' had been hastily cobbled together. It was made from bits of wood, decorated with bundles of wet grass and bunches of soggy flowers, and Angel realised that she was supposed to sit on it to perform her 'magic'. She climbed up and settled herself as best she could on the sodden seat, trying not to grimace as it squelched ominously under her. The rain trickled through her hair

84

and down her face. *Now what?* she thought. Was she supposed to say something? And if so, what on earth *could* she say?

Karma stepped in front of the 'throne', then, flinging both arms skyward, he launched into a stirring proclamation about Yellow Sun and Blue Skies and Green Leaves and Healing. The Villagers answered with cries or moans or whoops, depending on what was expected of them – then Karma swung round and gestured towards Angel.

'O, Spirit Childe! We, the Children of the Stars, Custodians of the Trees, Guardians of All Nature's Virtues, call upon you now to Work Your Magic and Heal Our Land! Cast your Spell, Spirit Childe – Cast it, and Let All Be Well Again!'

There was an awful, waiting silence. The Villagers' eyes seemed to bore through Angel like hot knives, and though their smiles were as sweet and friendly as ever, she felt as menaced as she had when the marauders had confronted her in the Experience Mart.

'Er . . .' she said.

'*Ahhhh!*' breathed the Villagers. '*Yes; oh, yes!*'

'Hush!' Karma commanded them sternly. 'The Spirit Childe must not be interrupted in her Great Magic!' And to Angel: 'Speak, O Spirit Childe! Speak in the Tongue of the Spirit Realm, and let the Rain and Sun Obey You!'

Angel felt as if her tongue had glued itself to the roof of her mouth. But then, as she groped desperately in the muddle of her mind, Karma's last words gave her a vital clue. *Speak in the Tongue of the Spirit Realm* – her only hope was to give them an impressive mouthful of words that would mean nothing whatever to them. This whole ceremony was so crazy that they probably *expected* her to talk gibberish. If she could just satisfy them for the moment, it would at least give her time to think up an excuse for failure.

She took a deep breath to steady her nerves, and said, 'Input: network communications.'

Another gasp went up. Everyone stood very still, staring; even Karma was mesmerised.

'Connect me to Zone Bohemia,' Angel went on. 'Vid link, Azure Block.'

'Spirit Magic!' someone whispered. 'Oh, she is so wise!'

Angel wrenched her face into a suitably stern expression. 'Spider off, or I'll wipe your circuits!' she announced portentously. Then suddenly she remembered her Therapet, Twinkle, and changing her voice to a fair imitation of Twinkle's goo-goo tone, she added, 'My sponsors are called Recreation Realm FunFriends, and I know a song about them. Shall I sing it for you now? It goes like this: "*I'm Just A Little FunFriend, FunFriend, FunFriend; I hope that you'll be My Friend, My Friend too!*" '

It was totally and utterly insane. As Angel sang Twinkle's fatuous song, the Villagers went into raptures. All the yelling and whooping that had gone before were nothing to what they did now: they jumped around like demented kids, rolled on the ground (covering themselves in mud and grass-stains in the process) and waved their arms or kicked their legs wildly in the air. Some started to bang and blow things in a kind of cacophonous music, and a few even started to chant the song's words, '*I'm Just A Little FunFriend, FunFriend, FunFriend*', as if they were the key to some fabulous spiritual awakening.

She didn't know how long the chanting and cavorting went on, but at last the Villagers must have had enough, for they started to collapse on the grass in a daze of happy exhaustion. Angel looked nervously round for Karma, but he was flaked out with the rest of them, flat on his back and staring up at the rain with a beatific grin on his face.

Oh, well. Phase One was safely completed, by the look of it. Phase Two — what to do when the magic didn't work — was a vid she'd play later, when she had had a chance to think. No one was paying any attention to her now, so she scrambled cautiously down from the dripping throne and, trying to appear both casual and dignified in case some people were looking, returned to the Dwelling.

As she went, she thought: *Winter, you'd better get back spidering quickly! Because if you don't, I think there could end up being some very big trouble around here!*

By the following morning, the rain had vanished and the sun shone in a cloudless sky.

Angel found out about it when three women, led by Sky, came rushing into her room not long after dawn and woke her up to tell her about the miracle she had wrought. Karma appeared soon afterwards and made an oily speech praising the Spirit Childe's Wisdom and Beneficence, then Angel was taken in triumph to the Dwelling's big central room for a very special communal Breakfast, at which everyone sang songs and kissed each other and the food was almost edible.

The coincidence was an astonishing piece of good luck. Angel even caught herself wondering if perhaps the Spirits that Karma was so fond of preaching about really did exist, and she had done something to please them. The notion was absurd and didn't last for long. But the change in the weather had effectively saved her skin – and the Villagers were more in awe of her than ever.

Halfway through the morning, the horse and cart was sighted on the valley track. A number of people ran to meet it; Angel wanted to run with them, but caution held her back. Nonetheless, as the procession approached she strained for a glimpse of Winter, and relief made her tingle when she spotted his distinctive white hair among the small crowd thronging round the cart.

They halted in the Village square, and at once the crowd swelled as people gathered to help with the unloading. The cart's axles were sagging under its cargo; piles of sacks that bulged at the seams, and an enormous heap of dark brown, stringy stuff that gave off a horrible smell. Angel held her nose and backed away, hiding behind one of the smaller huts where the reek didn't reach. A few minutes later, Winter came looking for her.

'Angel!' Glancing over his shoulder to make sure no one had seen him, he hurried to her side. Angel took a rapid step backwards, waving at the air in front of her face.

'You *stink*!' she said.

'So would you, if you'd spent two days wading around tide-flats,' Winter retorted. 'Look, I'm sorry, Angel – they sent me away so suddenly that there was no chance to tell you.' He was grimy and dishevelled as well as smelly, she saw now, his clothes salt-bleached and his hair as stringy as the brown stuff on the cart. And he looked desperately tired.

'Do·you think Karma arranged it deliberately?' Angel asked.

He shook his head. 'I wondered, but I don't think so. Except for that first time, he doesn't know we've talked to each other. No; it was just an unlucky coincidence.' His eyes met hers, keenly. 'Unlike the lucky one that's happened to you.'

'Oh,' she said. 'You've heard about it.'

'It was the first thing they told us.' He hesitated. 'What did you do?'

She described her frantic improvisation, expecting him to laugh. He didn't. Instead, his expression grew very serious and he said, 'You *were* lucky this time. But what happens when they want another miracle?'

Angel shrugged uneasily. 'Such as what?'

'It could be anything. Say there was another epidemic—'

'What's an epidemic?'

He looked shocked. 'You don't know?'

She shook her head. 'I've never heard the word. Should I have done?'

'I—' Then Winter thought better of what he was about to say. 'No. Maybe not, where you come from.' He sighed. 'I won't explain now. Too many people around – look, meet me at the waterfall, say . . . two hours after noon.'

'How will I know when that is?'

He studied the horizon. 'When the shadow of that tree touches the hedge. See it? Tell Karma that you want to Commune at the pool and that no one's to interrupt you. He'll fall for that, so we'll have the place to ourselves. I'd better go now, before I'm found with you.' He gave her a wry grin. 'And I promise I'll clean up in the meantime.'

Karma was obviously disappointed that the Spirit Childe did not want him to accompany her to the Pool of Spiritual Communion, but he accepted it with as good a grace as he could manage. When Angel arrived at the pool, Winter was already waiting. He did look cleaner, though the smell still clung to him, and without wasting any time he led Angel to the pool's edge.

'Can you swim?' he asked.

'Sort of.' Angel looked dubiously at the water. She didn't want to admit that her only experience of swimming was in Vee, where you didn't sink unless you wanted to and everything was warm and safe. This did *not* look safe. 'How deep is it?'

'Not very. Your feet can always touch the bottom.' Winter grinned. 'It might be a bit cold, though.'

It was. Angel yelped with shock as they plunged in; her teeth chattered and her legs went numb, and she stammered that it was the most horrible experience of her entire life. But after a minute or two she began to get used to it, and followed Winter as he waded towards the waterfall. It looked a lot higher and more alarming from within the pool, and the noise seemed colossal at very close quarters. Winter grasped her hand, told her to shut her eyes and hold her breath, and then pulled her right under the cascade. The tumbling water hit her head and shoulders like hammer blows; there was a great roaring in her ears, then, gasping and spluttering, she stumbled through to the inside of the fall.

'*Oh*!' Clinging to Winter as if he were a lifeline, she opened streaming eyes. Though the light under the waterfall was dim and green and flickering, it was enough to show the narrow fissure, taller than her own height, in the wet, moss-covered rock face. The pool had sloped up and the water was only thigh deep now.

Tugging at her hand, Winter said, 'Come on. It's just through here.'

His voice echoed hollowly, making her shudder. He towed her into the fissure, which seemed to close and squeeze in; a few paces and then suddenly the rock tunnel opened out again, and they emerged into a small cave. Light came in through vents in the cliff, showing up the uneven floor, and water dripped dismally from the roof.

And in the middle of the cave stood Winter's 'contraption'.

It *was* another mirror sculpture. In fact, it looked identical to the exhibit in the Experience Mart, except that there were no artfully placed streams of water playing over it. Angel walked all around it, peering at each mirror in turn, hoping – and half expecting – to see some fantastical change in the dim reflections. All she saw, though, was her own eager but baffled face gazing back.

After a while she touched it. It felt like plasglass, all

right; cold and very smooth; and it gave off – or did she imagine that? – a faint electrical tingle that resonated in her fingertips. Raking through her memory, she tried to conjure up a clear picture of the piece in the Mart. *Were* they both the same? Or were there some subtle differences – the number of mirrors, for instance? This one had eleven. She couldn't recall for certain how many the other had had, but thought it was more . . .

'When you saw my reflection,' she said to Winter, 'did anything else happen?'

He frowned. 'What kind of anything else?'

'I don't know: a change in the light, maybe. Or the colours.'

'No-o . . . I don't think so. Only – my hair was wet, of course, from the fall, and when I leaned over the mirrors, some water dripped on one of them.'

Water . . . the missing ingredient, Angel mused. Could that be a clue?

Winter was looking at her. 'Is this like the thing you saw in your world?' he asked.

'Yes, it is. But I don't know how it works, any more than you do.' One thing was sure, though. These sculptures were the key to the dimensional door through which she had been thrown. A door into time.

But did they – *could* they – work in both directions? And if they could, what would it take to activate them again?

She spent a few more minutes examining the mirrors, hoping for inspiration, but none came, and eventually there seemed no point in staying any longer. The return through the waterfall was slightly less shocking because she now knew what to expect, and they hauled themselves out of the pool and flopped down on the grass to let the sun dry their hair and clothes.

'The question is,' Winter said, 'how are we going to make that thing work?'

Angel didn't answer immediately. A new thought was nagging at her; it set her conscience stirring again, but she couldn't shake it off. Winter obviously wanted to use the mirrors to send her back home – but did *she* want that? Back to school; back to Soho and Cray and all the other people who claimed to know what was best for her, no matter what her own feelings might be. Back to the prospect of being Paired, like it or lump it, with that crawling fad-radical, Bright. She was getting used to Albion, and for all its primitiveness and weird customs, she was starting to like it. In a way it *was* very similar to her own Avalonne, but better, because it had a reality – of course – that Avalonne could never match.

Then there was Winter. Though they had only known each other for a few days, Angel could honestly say that he was the first real friend she had ever had. None of her co-educationates were remotely like him: they didn't understand Angel, and though they were nice enough to her face, she knew that they sneered at her behind her back. Winter wouldn't do that. Winter was open, honest; he *understood* her; because he, like her, was something of a misfit in his own world.

She sighed heavily, and didn't realise she was doing it until Winter said, 'What's the matter?'

Could she explain to him? Should she? Angel decided to try. But when she haltingly began, his face changed.

'Angel, you can't stay here,' he said. 'Not for ever.'

She looked at him unhappily, a little resentfully. 'Why not? I've got nothing worth going back for. Albion is—'

'Albion is going to get dangerous for you before much longer.'

She frowned. 'Why? I know you said the other day that Karma wouldn't be too pleased if he found out that I'm not a Spirit Childe; but why should he find out? I can hack his programme – look at what happened yesterday. He was really impressed!'

'Fine. So what if your magic *doesn't* work?'

She shrugged. 'I'll think up an excuse. Provided I stay one step ahead of him—'

'But you won't.' Winter moved restlessly. 'I tell you now, Angel, when the next epidemic comes, and he expects you to cure it, and you can't, and people start dying—'

'Hover a minute!' Angel interrupted, startled. 'What do you mean, *dying*?'

He stared at her for a very long time, and she couldn't read his expression; his face had closed, and there was pain behind the look in his eyes. Then at last he said: 'You don't know what an epidemic is. Well, I'll tell you. It's an outbreak of sickness that spreads through a Village. Then it reaches other Villages – it only takes one infected person to travel from one place to another. And people *die* of it.' Turning away, he scraped at the ground with a piece of twig he had picked up. 'Like my parents did.'

Angel stared at him in dawning horror. 'Your parents are . . . dead? *Both* of them?'

Winter nodded. He had been six years old when it happened, he told her. The disease had been brought to the Village by a group of outside visitors, and a total of nineteen people had died of it. Angel was shocked. In her world, people only died young if they spent too much time in the open air without the proper medical precautions, and the only ones who did that were the Vigilants, who had to, and the marauders, who chose to. Very occasionally there was a transcontinent shuttle accident, of course, but it was extremely rare, and anyway most people preferred to travel in Vee rather than physically, unless they absolutely had to, so they didn't run the risk in the first place. When someone *did* die unexpectedly it was major news, and almost the whole city went into trauma for weeks. Here, though, it seemed that early death happened to a lot of people, and it was accepted – almost expected, in fact. It was downright horrific.

'So,' said Winter at last, having shaken off her halting efforts to sympathise. 'Now you know what an epidemic is. Do you think you could cure one?'

With one call to SynergyMed, of course she could, Angel thought. Anyone could. But in this world, with no medics or medication, it was another story-vid entirely.

'No way,' she admitted.

'Right. But when another epidemic does start, Karma and the others will *expect* you to cure it. That's why you're here, after all – to perform Spirit Magic for the good of the Village. At the first sign of trouble they'll come running to you for help – and when you fail, they are *not* going to like it.'

'They'll realise that I'm a fake . . .' Angel said in a small voice.

'Maybe. Or maybe they'll think you're something else. If you're not a benevolent spirit, then the obvious conclusion is that you must be an evil one. And there's only one way to deal with evil spirits.'

'Which is?' she asked uneasily.

He didn't answer in words; he simply drew a finger across his own throat. The gesture would have been as unmistakable in her world as it was in his, and Angel blanched.

'You're winding me . . . aren't you?'

'No,' said Winter flatly. 'They've tried to do it before. A couple of years ago, a stranger came to the Village – he looked peculiar, and he wore weird clothes; not as weird as yours, but we'd never seen anything like them before. There was a crop failure that year, and he arrived when it was happening. So Karma decided he must be an evil spirit, and ordered him killed.' He hunched his shoulders. 'Luckily for the stranger, he got wind of it, and when they went for him he'd gone. But you might not be so lucky.'

A deep, cold shiver went through Angel, and she got up and paced back to the pool, where she stood staring down into the water. The thought that the Villagers could, and would, actually *kill* another human being was so appalling that she could barely grasp it. They were so kind, so gentle; weird, all right, but harmless. Or so she had believed. But if Winter was telling the truth, then under the surface they must all be as crazy as marauders.

She looked back at Winter over her shoulder, looked at his face, and knew that he was telling the truth. Struggling for something to blunt the savage edge of his revelation, she said, 'It might not come to that. These epidemics – they can't happen very often, or there'd be no one left alive by now.'

'That's true,' Winter agreed. 'But we heard some news while we were away, from another group we met at the salt flats. A village four days from here has started the Grey Rose sickness.'

Angel looked blank. 'Is that bad?'

'It's not just bad, it's one of the worst.' Winter hunched his shoulders. 'It starts with a headache that won't go away, then a fever that makes you sweat. Then you get blotches on your face and chest and under your arms; they look a bit like grey roses, which is how the sickness got its name. They get bigger, then they swell . . . and then, unless you're very lucky, you die.'

'And . . . and your people can't do anything about it?' she asked.

'No. None of our herbs have any effect. The only thing our healers can do is give the sick ones something to make them sleep, so they don't suffer too much.'

'Spiders . . .' Angel swore softly. 'That's *awful*.' She glanced nervously at him. 'You said this Village is four days away. Surely that's a safe enough distance?'

'Maybe; maybe not. It only takes one person to come in contact with one of the sick ones, then move on, meet someone from another place, and . . .' Winter shrugged, leaving the sentence unfinished.

Something crawled under Angel's skin. 'Like you met those people at the flats . . .'

'Exactly. They said they hadn't been near that Village. But I'm not sure they were telling the truth. One of them had a slight fever; and he kept rubbing his head when he thought no one was looking, as if he was trying to ease a pain.'

She shuddered, and stared down at the pool again. 'Could you . . . I mean, if he *was* starting the sickness . . . is it possible . . . that one of you might have caught it?'

There was a long pause. Then Winter said simply, 'Yes.'

Angel put the back of one hand against her mouth and shut her eyes tightly. She tried to tell herself that Winter was wrong: the stranger probably hadn't been incubating the disease, and even if he had, one brief contact couldn't be enough to pass it on. But, deep down, she knew she was deluding herself. Nothing was certain, true. But the worst was a deadly possibility.

She looked at Winter again, and her eyes were filled with worry that only just stopped short of fear.

'What are we going to do?' she asked him.

Winter was digging at the grass with the piece of twig again. He didn't meet her gaze. 'Wait,' he said. 'Just wait and see. There's nothing else we *can* do.'

EIGHT

Angel escaped to her room in the Dwelling as early as she prudently could that evening. Winter's warning had gone home with a vengeance, and she badly needed time to think.

Any romantic idea she had had about making a new life for herself in Albion had been wiped from her mind. There was no question that she had to find a way to escape back to her own world, and her only hope was the mirror structure behind the waterfall. Yet while that was all fine in principle, in practice it looked like an impossible conundrum. She knew, in theory, that the mirrors could transport her through time – but how to make them work?

She decided that her best approach was to try to remember *precisely* what had happened to her in those last moments in the Experience Mart. It wouldn't be easy; when you already had a gang of marauders to worry about, the fine details weren't exactly likely to be uppermost in your mind. But at Schol last term Cray had given some Retention seminars as part of the Objective Interaction programme. Angel had not paid much attention – earning herself yet another Offence mark in the process – but some of the exercises had sunk in. If she could recall them now, it might lead to something.

There was another, lesser worry at the back of her mind – Winter wanted to return to Zone Bohemia with her. Angel was alarmed at the prospect. For a start, she would never be able to explain him away to Soho or anyone else; and for another, the complications for any unregistered citizen in her world were horrendous. She had tried to explain matters to him, then, when he clearly didn't understand, she had tried to put him off with scare stories about everything from open-air pollution and marauders to the more immediate horrors of Interact and parental control. Winter was stubbornly unmoved: he wanted to go with her, and that was that. What, he argued, did he have to look forward to here? No one in the Village really cared about him; Karma allowed him to live in his Dwelling, but he had always been grudging about it, and never let Winter forget that he should be grateful. Angel's conscience had stabbed her at that, for she understood Winter's feelings all too well. As far as the Villagers were concerned, he was simply a nuisance, and that rang sympathetic chimes. So, goaded by a sense of guilt, she had let him talk her into a promise of sorts. If she failed to activate the mirrors, then of course the promise would have no meaning. But if she succeeded . . . well, Angel thought, she would just have to cope with that dilemma if and when it arose. In the meantime, at least she could count on Winter's willing help in solving the enigma of the time door.

But as days passed, they made no real progress. Angel was having trouble with the Retention exercises – for the first time in her life she wished that she had listened to

Cray's lectures – and her efforts to focus her memory on the fine details she needed were frustratingly slow and unreliable. She recalled that when she fell against the exhibit in the Experience Mart, she had twisted some of the mirrors out of place, so it seemed logical that the secret lay in the angle of the reflections. But the options were all but infinite: she and Winter could experiment for fifty years apiece and still not find the right combination. There *had* to be a short cut.

She returned again and again to the waterfall, hoping each time that some small thing, overlooked before, would give her inspiration. Nothing did. And, to complicate things further, Karma was starting to make a nuisance of himself. He was intrigued by the Spirit Childe's sudden preoccupation with the Pool of Spiritual Communion, and he very much wanted to know more. He didn't quite have the confidence to ask Angel any direct questions, but his hints were becoming broader and more frequent, and twice he had suggested that, as First Brother of the Village, he really should be permitted to accompany her on her visits now and then. Before long, Angel decided, she might have to allow him to come along, and invent some silly ritual to satisfy his curiosity and put him off the scent.

Before it came to that, though, the thing that she and Winter dreaded above all finally happened.

Five days had gone by since the seaweed- and salt-gathering party had returned to the Village. On the sixth morning, the party leader showed the first symptoms of the Grey Rose sickness.

Angel heard the news when she returned from yet

another foray to the waterfall before the Dwelling's communal breakfast hour. Bracing herself for another session of probing from Karma, she was met instead by Winter, who intercepted her just beyond the Village boundaries. His face was tense and he didn't waste words; he simply said, 'Morning's got the sickness.'

Angel stopped dead on the track. 'Oh, flackers . . . Are you sure?'

Winter nodded. 'He was complaining of a headache last night, and this morning it's worse, with a fever beginning.' He glanced quickly over his shoulder, nodding towards a squat, round building that stood alone some way apart from the rest of the Village. 'Karma's sent him to the Stricken House, but it won't do any good; he's already been with too many people. It's starting, Angel. Another epidemic.'

She started to move towards him, saying, 'What are we—' but hastily he backed away, holding up both hands with palms outward. 'Don't come any closer! I was with them too, remember.'

Angel paled. 'Winter, no—'

He made a negating gesture. 'It isn't certain I'll get it; some people don't, even when they've had close contact with the sick ones. But I don't want to take any chances. Angel, things are going to get dangerous for you now. Karma won't waste any time; he'll want the Spirit Childe magic, and he'll want it fast. Did you get anywhere at the fall this morning?'

Miserably, Angel shook her head. 'No. I've got a *sort* of a theory, but it's much too vague to even explain to you, let alone try out.'

'Vague or not, you might have to try it soon,' he said. 'Work on it, Angel – for the sake of the sun and moon, *work* on it. And if I can help—'

'Spirit Childe!' A voice called from the Village; looking past Winter, Angel saw Sky hurrying towards her and waving.

'Spirit Childe, Karma begs to speak with you!' she panted as she approached. 'Please – it's a matter of the gravest importance!' Suddenly Winter's presence registered, and her tone and expression both changed. 'What are you doing here?' she demanded. 'How dare you impose on the Spirit Childe; who do you think you are? Get away – and keep away from all of us, or Karma will put you in the Stricken House with Morning!'

Angel said, a little curtly, 'Winter wasn't imposing on me, Sky. He came to tell me of the – the tragedy.'

Sky flicked Winter another resentful glance. 'It isn't your place to tell the Spirit Childe anything!' Then she turned back to Angel and her face lit up. 'And of course it won't be a tragedy now. Because we know you'll help us, Spirit Childe. You'll cure Morning, and no one else will fall ill. We *know*!'

Looking at the crowd of faces in front of her, Angel felt herself sweating with terror and dread. The tension in the atmosphere was so powerful that she felt she could have reached out and grasped it by handfuls, and the silence gave her a sick, crawling sensation right down into her bones. They were waiting for a miracle. They *demanded* one.

Telling Karma that she needed to be alone to 'prepare for the Great Magic', Angel had spent all morning alone in her room, frantically planning a mock ritual that would impress the Villagers and buy her some time. She desperately wanted Winter with her, but of course that was out of the question. So with only her own wits to rely on, she decided that her best bet was to do what she had done before: a string of terminology and jargon from her own world that the Albionites would not understand. To add to the impact she had asked for certain flowers and leaves to be gathered, and a vast heap of them now lay before the 'Spirit Childe's throne' in the Village square. At noon – Angel hadn't the least idea when noon was, but someone would tell her – the Healing Rite was to begin.

The signal came, and Angel rose to her feet. It's impossible for silence to become *more* silent, but that, she felt, was what this silence did. The tension swelled . . . Shutting her eyes, and taking a shudderingly deep breath, Angel said in a loud, clear voice:

'INPUT. INTERNATIONAL COMMUNICA-TIONS: ZONE BOHEMIA TO EUROSTATE THREE . . .'

'It was good,' Winter said. 'They were impressed. But they're not going to stay impressed for long.' He glanced away from Angel, back down the track towards the village. 'Morning's worse. The sweating's started now, as well as the fever, and he can hardly bear the pain in his head.'

Angel bit her lip, staring at the waterfall tumbling unconcernedly down its rock face, and thinking of the enigma that lay behind it. She had spent the afternoon trying to work on her theory, but didn't seem to be getting much further. What she really needed to do was put it to the test, but that could be dangerous. If her idea was completely wrong, nothing would happen and so it wouldn't matter. But if – as was possible – she was *partially* right, then she could end up not in her own time but in another; past or future, absolutely *anywhere*. She didn't dare risk it.

She asked Winter, 'How long do you think we've got?'

'I don't know. Morning might recover – some people do – and then you could claim it was because of your magic. But if he doesn't, or if others get the sickness . . .' He shrugged.

'I told them it might take time,' Angel said, clutching at straws. 'I said I'd do two rituals every day, at noon and midnight, and that it would take a while for the magic to work.'

'Fine. But you can't go on like that for ever.'

They started to walk back down the track – this had been a secret meeting and it wouldn't do for either of them to be away from the Village for too long – and Angel felt his words weighing on her mind. She knew that they were true, but wished he hadn't said them. Something would have to give. Something would have to be done.

The trouble was, she didn't know if she could find the courage to do it.

Angel continued to perform her rituals, and by the

morning of the third day the situation was an uneasy hiatus. No one else had gone down with the sickness, but at the same time Morning was not getting better. He still lay in the Stricken House, tended by his daughter, Crystal, who was the only person willing to go near him. His condition had not deteriorated, but neither did it show any sign of improving.

Then, on the third day, the first grey blotches appeared on Morning's skin.

There was a desperate edge to Angel's next noon ritual, and when she finished, it seemed to her that the Villagers' attitude towards her was beginning to change. Hints of doubt, suspicion and mistrust were creeping in, and it was all too easy to imagine what they were whispering behind her back. *The Spirit Childe has failed us. Her magic is not working.*

Time was running out.

By evening, Crystal had gone down with the disease. Angel fluffed and improvised her way through the midnight ceremony. She went to bed with the Villagers' reproachful looks stinging in her memory, and had awful dreams.

She was woken long before dawn by a voice hissing her name.

Angel opened her eyes, puzzled. The voice seemed to have come from some way off; it had sounded like Winter, but in the dark she could make out nothing. Then her vision adjusted and she saw him, a vague silhouette at the far side of the room.

'Winter?' She whispered. 'What is it, what's happened?'

He said, in a strange, unsteady tone, 'Morning's dead. And . . . my head *hurts* so much . . .'

'Come on!' she said. 'I know it hurts, I know you just want to lie down and rest, but you've *got* to keep going!'

Winter's only answer was a groan, followed moments later by a sudden thud, as if something heavy had been dropped on the ground. Angel groped her way back through the pre-dawn gloom, and found him lying prone on the track. He was clutching at his skull, and when she tried to pull him to his feet he protested, 'I c-can't . . . oh, Angel, I'm so *cold* . . .'

Angel swore through gritted teeth. How much farther was it to the waterfall? If only she could *see* properly! She would have given anything for a proper handbeam, or even a nightglow; she had brought a candle, but the wind had blown it out almost immediately they were clear of the Village and she didn't know how to make it light again. Winter could have helped her. But right now, it was more than he could do to stay upright.

She was horrified by the speed at which the symptoms of the Grey Rose sickness had come on. Last night, when she had performed her ritual, he had been in the crowd and he had seemed as well as ever; but in the space of a few hours had come this violent change.

And it had changed all Angel's plans and resolves. With Morning's death, the time she had bought with her phony 'magic' had finally run out. She couldn't wait any longer: she *had* to try to get away from Albion. And she couldn't leave Winter behind to die.

Angel had never thought of herself as a particularly caring person. Everyone from Soho to Cray told her that she was selfish and ungrateful, and she had developed a defensive response that said; Fine, if that's what they expect then I'll live up to their expectations. Winter had changed that. Winter was a friend, her first *real* friend, and she would *not* abandon him.

'Come *on*!' she said again, anger in her voice. 'I'm not doing it all for you! Get up, Winter; get *up*!'

With an enormous effort Winter managed to stagger reasonably upright at last, and, supporting him under the arms, she pulled him slowly and awkwardly onwards. The sky was a shade lighter now, which was good and bad: good because she would be able to see better soon, bad because it wouldn't be long before Karma discovered that the Spirit Childe had flitted out on him. Another half hour and the Village would be in an uproar. The search would be on – and the waterfall would be one of the searchers' first targets.

She heard the fall before she saw it, and her heart turned painfully over with sheer relief. From slate grey the sky had by now turned pearly, and the tumbling water glowed eerily in the gathering light, like something out of a mindbending holo. Winter was hardly moving his feet by now, and Angel all but dragged him to the edge of the pool. She only hoped that the shock of a plunge into cold water would shake him up enough to get them both through. If it didn't, and he slipped and went under, she wouldn't have the strength to pull him out . . .

Luckily, the shock did revive him, and together they

stumbled and spluttered through the fall, emerging into the cave on the other side. Here, it was almost pitch dark again, but that no longer mattered. They were safe from discovery in the cave, and the rock vents that let in light faced almost due east. All they had to do was wait until the sun rose.

The wait felt endless. Winter drifted into an uneasy, feverish sleep, but Angel huddled on the cave floor, trying not to think about how cold and wet she was. At first she counted the minutes passing, but she kept losing track of her counting, and anyway, it only made time drag out and seem far longer. Then, at last, a glimmer of light began to creep into the cave from above, and when she looked up, she saw the rose and gold of sunrise reflecting on the rocks high above her head. The shape of the mirror device was forming slowly out of the gloom; she could see its outlines now, and the first reflections in the plasglass, and—

Angel frowned as she realised suddenly that the mirrors didn't look quite as she remembered them. Something was out of kilter, different . . . With a quick glance to ensure that Winter was still breathing, she struggled to her feet (her legs were numbed by the cold and wouldn't work properly) and stumbled across the uneven floor to look more closely.

The device *had* changed. Angel knew it as surely as she knew anything, for in the past few days she had examined the mirrors so many times that the picture of them was firmly imprinted on her mind. Somehow, the angles had been altered.

And then, with a flick of clarity so powerful that it

made her gasp aloud, the memory she had been struggling and failing to unlock came slamming back. The Experience Mart, the marauders, the terror of falling forward into the sculpture – *this was exactly how the mirrors had looked at that moment!*

'Winter! Winter, wake up!' She grabbed his shoulders unceremoniously and shook him so hard that he was jolted out of his feverish stupor.

'Wha——?' he began muzzily, but she didn't give him time to ask any more. 'Come on, come *on*! The mirrors, the light – everything's right! Come *on*, Winter, *hurry!*'

He was too far gone to comprehend fully, but her urgent voice rallied him, and on hands and knees he crawled across the floor to the device. Angel was fumbling for the other piece of equipment she had brought; a soft leather bottle, the largest she had been able to find in the frantic, furtive minutes before they fled from the Village. Locating it, she scrabbled to the edge of the pool and filled it with water. When she returned, Winter had raised himself on his hands and was staring, stupefied, at the device. An unsteady hand reached out——

'No!' Angel warned. 'Don't touch it – leave it exactly as it is!' Raising the bottle, she held it poised above the sculpture. This was the missing factor; the extra ingredient that the exhibit in the Experience Mart had had——

A stream of water poured from the bottle and splashed over the sculpture. The light from overhead turned the stream to silver, and as it fell on the mirrors it was as though they lit up from within. Angel's memory gave another huge lurch; she shook the bottle, turning the

110

stream to a splashing cascade. Light flared in the mirrors; she saw her own face, Winter's beside her with eyes closed and mouth slack. A rainbow of colours flared, seemed to swell towards her; her balance went, she clutched convulsively at Winter's arm—

And, but for the mirror sculpture, the cave was empty.

Or seemed to be . . . until a shadow moved among shadows, in a deep recess where the shafts of daylight couldn't reach. It didn't show itself, not clearly. But the hand that reached out would just have been visible through the gloom, if anyone had been there to see it. The hand touched the mirrors, made a tiny adjustment to one angle, another, and a third. It hovered briefly, as though its owner was debating whether or not to do any more. Then it withdrew. And the shadow was no longer there.

Soft, jingling music swam into Angel's consciousness like one of the house Whirligig's relentless wakeup calls. The floor beneath her was as hard as it had been moments ago, but it was also smooth, quite unlike rock. And the air was *warm*.

Hardly daring to hope, she opened her eyes.

She was lying on the floor of the Experience Mart's exhibition gallery. Soft, artificial light played gently on her face, perfumed air wafted past her nostrils. Winter lay unmoving beside her. And a few centis from them both, the mirror device with its cunningly placed jets of water stood shining innocently on its plinth.

Angel sat up very slowly. She said nothing; all she could do at this moment was stare, drinking in the Mart's familiar colours and contours, listening to the jingling music, which stopped every few moments to deliver 'Today's Happythought, brought to you by the Hamamoto-Empathy Corporation, and wishing all our friends and customers the most *joyous* of mornings'. There was no one but herself to hear today's Happythought, which meant that it must be early; too early for people to be out of their cribs. No Vigilants or Mart guards in the area, either. So no one had seen their spectacular arrival.

But they *had* arrived. Angel had done it. The time door had worked again, and she was home.

Winter moaned then, and the sound jolted her out of her daze. Looking at him, she saw that he was still sprawling flat on the floor; he seemed to be trying to move, but he was no longer capable. Sweat streaked his white hair and trickled down the back of his neck, and abruptly Angel's common sense snapped back into place.

She rolled over quickly and raised her left arm, touching a code into the implanted control strip. A green light came on in the strip, and breathlessly she gasped, 'Input: network communications.'

There was momentary pause, then a tinny computer voice from her arm replied, 'Acknowledged, Angel Ashe.'

'Connect me with Synergymed; Aid and Remedy team.'

Another pause, then: 'Adult Authorisation needed.'

Angel could have screamed. 'This is an *emergency*!' she snarled at it.

'Adult Authorisation needed,' the computer repeated implacably.

'Oh, *pigs!*' She was home all right: she should have known, should have remembered the tight hold that Soho kept on her. *Calm down, Angel; calm down* . . . 'All right.' She clenched her fist in an effort to hold her temper in place. 'Then connect me with Soho Ashe, Azure Block, Zone Bohemia. And *hurry!*'

The computer probably did hurry, but all the same it seemed an age before Soho was woken and came on the link. When she did, though, her voice was shaking with fury.

'Who is this?' she shrilled. 'Who's using my daughter's vid-ident without authorisation? If this is the media again, then I warn you, my lawyer—'

Angel drew a huge breath and cried, '*Mother!*'

NINE

The shriek that Soho let out across the comm link was so loud that Angel's whole arm vibrated with the force of it. Amid a volley of sobs, yelps, scoldings and gushing relief, she was able to get the basics of the situation across to her mother, and was hysterically told to 'Wait there, wait, wait, *WAIT*, don't move a *CENTI* from where you are!' while Soho organised what sounded like an entire rescue squad to home in on her location. They started to arrive within minutes: first a team from the Mart's own security, then a pair of Vigilants, then a dox, two counsellors and a carer from SynergyMed, and lastly, in a frantic whirl of flowing black chiffonize and blue and green ringlets (she'd changed her hair again), Soho herself, who smothered Angel with hugs and kisses before fainting artistically on the floor. Angel finally managed to draw someone's attention to Winter, who still lay stunned where he had fallen; abruptly, then, the dox took charge of the situation, and suddenly they were being hurried to a waiting preserver-bubble that whisked them away to the nearest SynergyMed facility.

At the facility, Angel and Winter were instantly separated and taken to diagnostic cubicles. Angel's was soothing blue, with supposedly reassuring music and calming patterns playing across the walls. She kept trying to tell the dox that Winter was seriously ill and needed help, but everyone only said bland things like, 'Don't worry, everything's fine, you'll be double-A in no time', while connecting her up to stimulators, medicators, monitors and every other gadget imaginable. Angel dreaded to think how much it must all be costing, and wondered who in Tokyo was going to pick up the bill for Winter.

She had another problem where Winter was concerned, and that was, how to explain about him? The deluge of assorted medications that the dox was giving her had started to make her drowsy, but she rallied her brain and tried to think. The obvious answer wasn't long in coming, and it was Soho who started her on the right track. Soho hadn't been allowed into the cubicle, but Angel could hear her voice outside; recovered from her faint, she was talking loudly and dramatically to someone, but the cubicle walls muffled the sound and Angel couldn't hear most of what was being said. Only one phrase did catch her ear. 'Days and days and *days*!' Putting on a pathetic and helpless face, Angel turned to look at the dox.

'Please . . .' she said. 'What date is it . . .?'

The dox told her, and it was the clue she needed. She had, it seemed, been away from home for the same number of days that she'd been in Albion. So time had passed at the same pace in both worlds. *Good*, Angel thought. They hadn't asked her, yet, where she had been and what had happened to her; when they did, she would tell them that she had been abducted by marauders, and while in captivity she had met Winter, who was a fellow prisoner. She would claim that Winter had lost his memory – shock, sickness; the dox would find half a million logical reasons for it — and that would account for his peculiar ways and for the fact that he had no home to be sent back to. The carers would tie themselves in knots trying to trace his Prime Parent, and when they failed they'd have to do something to help him. Problem solved. All Angel had to do was make sure that Winter knew the strategy and would co-operate.

She drifted off to sleep soon afterwards, with the soothing music tinkling in her ears.

When she woke, she could still hear Soho talking. Her voice sounded closer now, though — and as Angel's mind swam slowly up into consciousness, she became aware of a light dancing on the far side of her closed eyelids.

'What is that . . .?' She opened her eyes a crack, then shut them again as the light homed in on her. A voice she didn't recognise said, 'Lovely, *lovely*! Keep that look, sweetie, yes, that's it, *perfect*!' and then the dox's voice intervened crossly, saying that that was enough and the client must be left alone now or she'd risk going into trauma, and that was expensive as well as detrimental to her wellbeing. The strange voice replied in a way that didn't sound too polite; there was a brief, muttered dispute, with Soho (of course) joining in; then abruptly the light vanished and footsteps went away, out of the cubicle.

'Darling?' A shadow fell over Angel and Soho's tone dripped compassion. 'Darling, can you hear me?'

'Yes, Soho,' said Angel, remembering just in time to sound weak and vague, and wondering who the person with the light had been.

'Open your eyes, darling; let me look at you and make sure you're all right,' Soho urged. Angel opened them, and was rewarded with the sight of her mother's face framed in its blue and green ringlets. Tears were glittering like myriad tiny crystals on her eyelashes, which were three times longer than normal, and she had had a new face-make that gave her a subtle but carefully emphasised pallor.

She clasped her hands together and breathed, 'Oh, my precious Angel, where have you *been*?'

Angel's performance then would, she decided, have landed her a lead part in a drama-vid, if only there had been a vid-maker there to see it. Haltingly, and with plentiful lip-trembles and shuddering sighs, she reeled off a wonderfully confusing tale of kidnap and terror and mayhem. Soho's responses were very gratifying; she gasped and cried and wrung her hands in all the right places, finally declaring melodramatically to the dox that Her Child had 'Suffered an Abominable Ordeal, and Nothing, *Nothing* must be spared in the Quest to Rehabilitate Her.' She sounded just like Karma.

As Soho took a break between declamations, Angel said (feebly), 'Soho . . . is Winter all right . . .?'

'Winter?' Soho repeated. 'Who's Winter?'

'The boy . . . He helped me, Soho. He was so kind . . .'

'What boy?' Soho looked thoroughly baffled. 'I didn't see any boy.'

'There was a boy with her,' one of the carers put in. 'He's in another cubicle undergoing treatment and therapy.'

117

Soho became alarmed and indignant. 'You mean she wasn't alone? Why didn't anyone *tell* me about this? Who is he? If he's one of those marauders—'

'He isn't!' Angel protested. 'They'd abducted him, too. Only he's lost his memory, and − and then he got ill, and—'

'Ah!' said the dox, turning round from his examination of a monitor. 'That probably explains it.'

'Explains what?' Soho demanded.

'His behaviour.' From the corner of her eye Angel saw the dox raise his eyebrows and tap a finger against the side of his own head. 'The child talks absolute fict. He was delirious when he was brought in, but it was only a mild fever and a couple of shots put it right. But we still can't make much sense of anything he says. Traumatic amnesia. That fits the slot.'

'Oh,' said Soho. 'Well, who is he? Has his Prime Parent been contacted?'

'Rather difficult,' said the dox with heavy patience, 'if he doesn't know who he is.'

'He can only remember his first name,' Angel supplied, hoping that that was plausible in traumatic amnesia cases. 'Perhaps if I could talk to him . . .?'

'Later, maybe,' said the dox. 'He's sleeping now. And so should you be.'

Soho had a look on her face that Angel recognised; it meant she was thinking something over, weighing it up in her mind. 'If the boy *has* lost his memory . . .' she mused.

'He *has*,' Angel insisted.

'Yes, darling, so you said; I was just thinking aloud. If he

118

doesn't get it back, then we should help him, don't you agree?'

Angel was taken aback. It wasn't at all like Soho to be so benevolent. 'Yes,' she said quickly, before her mother could change her mind. 'I'd like that.'

'Oh, *good*. It's the humanitarian thing to do, isn't it? Of course it is! So you have some more sleep, darling, like the dox says, and I'll go and see about making some arrangements for the poor boy.' She switched on a beaming smile that encompassed everyone in the cubicle, and started for the door.

Angel called after her. 'Soho – does Kim know I'm all right?'

'Mmm?' Soho paused and looked back. 'Kim? Well, I expect so, darling. I'm sure someone will have put a comm through to him by now. I'll check. Have a vitalising sleep, my precious Angel – what is it Bright says? "I'll catch your sparkle later!" '

And she was gone.

Angel was finally allowed to see Winter the next morning. She had spent the intervening hours in the hands of the dox, who had had a wonderful time performing ever more elaborate checks on her health. She was tested for infection, contagion, trauma, aberration, hallucination, cognition, synaptic dysfunction, Societal Adjustment – every possible condition Angel could think of, and quite a few that she couldn't. Eventually she was pronounced double-A fit (she suspected that the dox was secretly disappointed not to have a challenge on his hands) and told that Soho would be coming that afternoon to take 'you both' home.

'Both?' said Angel.

'That's right. Winter's going with you — your Prime Parent has very generously offered him space in your apartment until his own people can be traced.'

Angel was boggled. Soho, *offering* space? It was *completely* unlike her, and on her one further, brief visit to the cubicle she hadn't mentioned a word about it. Oh, well. It would save Angel a lot of time and energy trying to persuade her.

There were quite a few people hanging round the far end of the facility corridor when Angel was escorted along to Winter's cubicle, and among them she saw several sporting the logos of Infax and W?W?W? (What? Where? Why?), the two major investigative news corporations. Supposing that some celeb was in the facility for a makeover or whatever, she thought no more of it and didn't give them a second glance.

Winter was very glad indeed to see her. Whatever the Albionites' Grey Rose sickness was, it had been no match for SynergyMed, and his fever was completely gone. He had also been bathed, given new clothes and had his hair styled — now he looked no different from any other citizen. He, like Angel, had had tests. A lot of them, and very thorough.

'I can't understand half the things they say to me,' he told Angel worriedly when the carer had left them alone. 'And all these things — lights and noises and pictures moving on the walls — if this is the future, then it's weird.' He shivered. 'It scares me.'

'You'll get used to it,' she told him. 'Like I got used to Albion . . . well, sort of, anyway. But listen, Winter, there's something I've got to tell you.' She explained about the amnesia idea and the marauders story. Winter seemed to grasp most of it; enough, anyway, to ensure that he would go along with the fict and keep the dox fooled. He would play the part of the lost waif, and if they asked him about things he didn't understand, he would act dumb.

'But what'll happen when they don't trace my parents?' he asked.

'They'll come up with all sorts of theories to explain it. Don't worry: no one's going to hurl you out on the streets or anything. You'll be looked after.'

'Like I was in the Village?' There was a sad, faintly bitter edge to his voice, and Angel looked away.

'No,' she said. 'Not like that. Here, you've got someone who does actually care about you.' Then, because the expression on his face made her want to lighten the subject, she added, 'Anyway, haven't they told you? I'm going home this afternoon, and you're coming too, to stay with us.'

'Us?'

'Me and Soho – my Prime – I mean, my mother.'

'Oh,' he said. 'Is that who she was? She came to see me yesterday, after the healers said I was cured.'

'Did she?' Angel was surprised yet again by Soho's interest. Or perhaps she had simply been curious.

'Yes. She talked to me; though I don't know what most of it meant.' He looked to one side of the crib, and nodded.

121

'She brought me all those things, too. I thanked her, but I don't know what I'm supposed to do with them.'

Angel looked. There was a face-make kit, a couple of holo games and several vids, most of which looked like fashion-trawling links except for one adventure fict and a docu-tour guide about the delights of Zone Bohemia. Presents, for a complete stranger? Soho really *was* on a new String route!

The aperture opened at that moment, and the carer came back. 'All double-A?' she asked chirpily, then without giving either of them a chance to answer went on, 'There's a Vee coming through for you, Angel. It's Kim, in Beijing.'

Kim — and on Vee! Angel leaped to her feet and followed the carer at a run to the nearest comm link. She slammed the connector into place so hard that she nearly broke it, and there was Kim, holding out his arms to her.

'Dad!' Kim wasn't like Soho; he didn't mind her calling him by a parental name, provided she didn't do it too often. They hugged, and she garbled the gist of her story to him while he called her honey and sweetheart and kookie and a lot of other endearments. At last, though, Kim broke off the embrace and stepped back with a smile.

'I can't hover too long, kookie. Pressures of work — got to get back online in a min.'

Her face fell. 'Can't you come to 'State-8 and see me in realtime?' she asked. 'Or — or why don't I shuttle over to you? I've never been to Beijing, and—'

'Beijing looks just like any other city, hon. Anyway, you've trawled it in Vee, and that's just as good, isn't it?'

'But—'

'Listen, sweetie, I've got to *go*. Busy-busy-busy, you know how it scans? I know you're safe now, and everything's double-A, so that's what matters, uh? I'll vid you at home tonight, if I can. Hugs and kisses, kookie — 'bye, now!'

Angel trailed back to Winter's cubicle with her spirits locked in a dull box and buried somewhere far underground. Winter saw her face and said, 'Is something wrong?' but she only shook her head. She couldn't explain, and didn't want to talk about it. She couldn't even get excited about going home; not any more.

But go home she did, that afternoon. It cheered her up a little to find that Soho had hired a private autonet rather than using the String, and the three of them returned to Zone Bohemia in style. Winter didn't utter a sound on the journey, and every time Angel looked at him, his eyes were tightly shut, as if the trip terrified him. He would certainly take some time to adjust, she thought.

There was a small crowd of people waiting at Azure Block's autonet link. Angel didn't realise the significance of that at first; she merely assumed that they were net customers waiting for a car. But then she saw the logos. The lights. The soundpix recorders in people's hands . . .

Soho all but pushed her out of the car, and straight into a dazzle and fusillade of questions.

'This is W?W?W?, Angel! How does it feel to be home?'

'Say something for our Infax customers, Angel — What did the marauders do to you?'

'How many traumatic episodes did you suffer?'

'How did you escape, Angel? Were you brave, or were you scared? Terraventurers all want to hear your story!'

'This way, Angel; look this way!'

'Tired, yeah – tired and frightened! Brilliant, fabulous; give us that expression again!'

Light, noise, babbling, whooping voices – Soho was in the thick of it, laughing and crying and posing and absolutely revelling in the attention. Angel could only stand frozen, while Winter, silent and wide-eyed with horror, gripped her arm; until, when one of the newsdrones shoved a light right in her face and demanded eagerly, 'What are your *emotions* at this moment in time?', her paralysis cracked.

'No . . .' she protested. 'No, please – not now; I can't – I just want to go *home!*'

She was allowed to go, eventually. As the bubble-lift sped them up to their floor, she leaned against the thruplast wall, trying not to burst into tears. She hadn't expected the media barrage, hadn't been *ready* for it, and the shock was almost more than she could take. Soho was saying cheerfully upbeat things about how exciting it all was and what fun it would be to see themselves on the newsvids, but Angel didn't listen. She felt fingers touch hers and tighten around them, and glanced at Winter with mute gratitude. He must have been fifty times more shocked than she was, but he seemed to be coping now. He just wanted to support her, and if Soho hadn't been there, she would have hugged him.

She feared that there would be more newsdrones outside the apartment, but Azure Block's security people had done their work, and they finished their journey unmolested. Inside the apartment, Angel wanted to run straight to her room, hurl herself into her crib and stay there until the world went away. She didn't. Instead, she stood numbly in the middle of the main salon, staring at the wall but seeing nothing.

A loud *bleep* snapped her out of it, and she looked up to see the house Whirligig bouncing gently through the air towards her.

'Oh, good,' said Soho. 'The 'gig's new functions are working properly. Did I tell you, darling; while you were lost, I had this facility programmed into it, so that it senses when anyone gets home and comes to meet them? It cost a fortune, of course, but the sponsors . . . Angel, are you listening?'

'I'm tired,' said Angel. 'May I go to my room?'

'Of *course* you may. But don't you want to help your friend get settled first? Show him all the consoles and everything? And I expect he's hungry; boys always are. Why not programme him some Nature's Kisses? It's very nutritious and he obviously needs nutrition, doesn't he? Or better still, I'm sampling a new range of products for Immedi-Eat; they're really *as*, and absolutely delumptious!' As she spoke she had wafted to the house computer console, and one perfect fingernail flicked over a blinking light. The computer announced, 'Seventeen communications have been received and stored, Soho; twelve vid, five Vee.'

'Oh, Tokyo!' Soho said disgustedly. 'The media again – I simply haven't *time* to deal with it all now; I've got to see Roma in half an hour—'

'See who?'

'Roma – oh, of course; you haven't met her yet. She's my new make adviser; totally superb and *so* talented; it's quite supernatural the way she knows *exactly* what's right . . . But she doesn't do house calls, and she has awful trauma if her clients aren't on time. I'm going to see if I can persuade her to take you on, too, darling; I'm sure she'll be willing under the circumstances . . .'

A small, mechanical part of Angel's brain listened as Soho chattered on, but the only thing that really registered was the fact that her mother was going out, and she and Winter would have a few hours alone. She waited impatiently while Soho told the computer to hold all the messages and order an autonet car, and within minutes she had departed in a flurry of waves and blown kisses and instructions to help themselves to *anything* they wanted.

The aperture closed with a faint hiss, and Angel felt her knees sagging. In an odd, flat voice, she said to Winter, '*Are* you hungry?'

He didn't answer, and when she looked at him he was standing in the middle of the floor, both hands covering his eyes, his shoulders shaking. Angel had the uneasy impression that he was laughing and crying at once, and that blend was something very close to hysteria.

She glanced at the 'gig, which was still hovering at a discreet distance. 'I want a meal,' she said. 'Something very plain.' The comm indicator on the house console bleeped. She ignored it. 'And two Silver Raindrops glitter-ices.'

'ACKNOWLEDGED,' the 'gig said obligingly. It changed colour briefly then added, 'PROGRAMMED.

MEAL READY IN FIVE MINS.'

Winter didn't object or resist when Angel propelled him to a couch and made him sit down. He was still covering his face and she didn't argue with that; her world was far, far too much for him to take in all at once, and he was probably trying grimly to hold on to his sanity. Food might help: at least it was a reference point of sorts. And she had never met anyone who didn't like glitter-ice.

A scratching noise came from behind the aperture that led to her own room. Frowning, Angel went to investigate, and when she opened the aperture, a small, gold-and-silver shape moved at her feet.

'Hello, Angel,' a childish little voice intoned. 'I've missed you, Angel. Will you be my friend?'

Twinkle, the Therapet, was gazing up at her with enormous green eyes that were filled with a combination of sadness and hope. Soho must have brought the Therapet home from the fateful party, but had forgotten to switch her off. Angel's own eyes brimmed suddenly with tears and, bending, she scooped up Twinkle in her arms and hugged her arti-fur body.

'Oh, Twinkle!' Her voice cracked and she felt a perfect idiot; but only Winter could hear, and Winter would understand. 'Twinkle . . . what's going to happen to us all now?'

TEN

What was going to happen – certainly if Soho had anything to do with it – was not at all what Angel had foreseen, and certainly not what she wanted. Because, like it or not, from the moment the media got wind of her return, she was a celebrity.

It had started, she discovered, soon after her disappearance. Soho, as hysterical as expected, had screamed kidnap and murder, and as such things didn't happen often in 'State-8, it wasn't long before the media picked up the story. Vids of Angel had been flashed firstly all over the city, then Statewide and even Eurowide, and when the best efforts of everyone from the Vigilants to media-sponsored private 'tecs failed to find any trace of her, the newsdrones had focused on the dramatic mystery angle. Angel's sudden and unexpected return, coupled with the fict she had invented about her 'escape', was a dream come true – and within twenty-four hours it wasn't only the news corporations that were involved. Eleven of the seventeen comms waiting for Soho when she had come home that first evening were offers from fict-movie makers, chatter-show producers and would-be sponsors of 'Angel Ashe, the Audacious Abductee' (alliteration was an *as* thing at the moment). Every one, of course, was offering big fees. Soho was over the stars, and couldn't for the world see why Angel wasn't as thrilled as she was.

'Darling, it's the opportunity of your *life!*' she said when she came into Angel's room late that night and woke her up from what should have been a sound sleep. 'Just *think* – you'll be on every vidwall from here to New New Delhi and back; there'll be interviews, shows, re-lives, games – there's one corporation talking about a Vee-movie, so people can share your ordeal and escape! And the *sponsorship!*' Soho clasped her hands and shut her eyes ecstatically. 'I've even had a comm from Hamamoto-Empathy! *Hamamoto-Empathy*, darling! They are the very *biggest*, and they're offering skies and *skies* of things! Angel, you could try for centuries and never get a chance like this!'

Angel knew that was true. But though she tried with all her energy over the next two days, she couldn't make Soho understand that she did not *want* skies and skies of things, from the Hamamoto-Empathy Corporation or anyone else. All she wanted was to be left to get on with her life in peace. But that, it seemed, was completely out of the question.

The only consolation in the midst of all the tumult was that Schol, and Cray, were now things of the past. Naturally, Soho said, it was completely out of the question for her to go back into Education; there simply weren't enough hours in the day for *everything*. Her First Pairing plans had been wiped, too. Once, Angel did tentatively ask about Bright, dreading what the answer might be. Soho, looking puzzled, said, 'Who, darling? Oh – oh, *him*. No, no, no, of course there's no question of a Pairing with Bright! I mean, really, he's *nobody*.'

'But I thought you and York were—' Angel began,

'Don't be silly, darling!' Soho interrupted hastily. 'York and I aren't anything; we never were. He isn't my type, and Bright certainly isn't yours. Not *now*.'

So First Pairing, it seemed, was off the agenda, at least for the time being. It helped. But it didn't solve any of Angel's other problems.

Her biggest worry of all was Winter. Though he tried his best to fit in, and to gain at least some grasp of the way Angel's world worked, she knew that he wasn't succeeding. The vivid noise and pace of the city scared and disorientated him, and the media attention was straining him towards the point where something was going to break. No one else noticed the signs, or if they did, they put it down to the aftermath of his trauma. After all, everyone had seen his pale, scared face staring out of the newscasts or stammering nearly inaudible replies to the drones' probing questions. He had been hustled on to two chatter-shows to 'rewind his experience' for avid subscribers, and the Terraventure network was pressing him to co-operate with Angel in a full-scale re-live for a worldwide 'cast. The Vee-movie people were impatient to get a contract sewn up – and Soho was getting impatient, too; Angel and Winter must surely, *surely* see that they wouldn't get a better offer if they waited for the sun to go nova. Angel still resisted, but she knew she wouldn't be able to hold out for ever. Soho was her Prime Parent and, ultimately, had control of her. When her patience finally ran out – which it would – then all she had to do was sign the contract herself on Angel's behalf, and that would be that.

Angel's one thread of hope was the fact that there was still great public interest in tracing Winter's next of kin. While that particular fict still ran, she could use the excuse that he wasn't empowered to sign any contracts. But the media would get bored eventually, and when they did, someone somewhere would pull a few strings and have him officially designated Unparented. They would put him up for adoption, and Soho would be first in the queue, unless one of the ever-growing list of sponsors beat her to it.

Finding opportunities to talk to Winter was becoming increasingly difficult as days went by. The apartment was constantly bombarded by callers, on vid, Vee and even in person, and on the few occasions when they could have snatched a few minutes alone together, Winter was reluctant to make use of them. He was increasingly withdrawn; almost hostile towards Angel, or so she sometimes felt. She couldn't get through to him, and she couldn't persuade him to tell her why.

At last, though, a good chance came. Angel and Winter had spent the morning with Roma, the make adviser, who had been persuaded to overcome her distaste for house visits by the thought of being linked with a big-time celeb. She was blueprinting an entire new look for them both, to be debuted on a new chatter-show called Heartbreak Hell in which Soho was to tell her Prime Parent's Anguish story again, while Angel and Winter sat beside her and 'gave emotional support'. Soho, whose own new look had already been completed, was at rehearsal in the vid-studio on the other side of the city, and Angel had discovered the knack of disabling the house console's alert function, so that incoming comms would be stored without bothering anyone in the apartment. Even the Whirligig had been persuaded to stop plying them with food, drinks, slogans, jingles and Happythoughts. For once, just for once, they had some peace.

So when Roma left and Winter started to head for his room, Angel stopped him.

'Winter, we've got to talk,' she said desperately.

He shrugged. 'What is there to say?'

'There's *skies* to say, spider it!' she fired at him. 'And I've been trying to say it for days, only you won't listen!'

Winter shook his head as though it hurt. 'I *can't* listen to any more!' he said. 'There's so much *noise*, so much *coming* at me all the time – I can't take it, Angel!' He looked at her. 'It's all right for you. This is your world, and you grew up with it. But it isn't mine. All the people, the – the sponsors and corporations and shows and vids and attention – I know you're enjoying it. But me . . . I just want to go home.'

Angel stared at him, stunned. 'You think I'm *enjoying* this?'

'Well, aren't you? It's what you're used to, after all.'

'But it isn't! Or if it is, then I don't want it, any more than you do!' She paused, on the brink of adding something and asking herself if it really was true. She decided it was. 'I want to get out of here, too. I want to come back to Albion with you.'

'You do?' It was Winter's turn to stare. Angel nodded.

'There's nothing for me here,' she said. 'Albion was – it

was *peaceful*, like Avalonne.' She had shown Avalonne to Winter, and once he was accustomed to the Vee-connect procedures he had enjoyed it as much as she did. As he had said, it felt much more like home.

'I don't care if Albion's primitive,' she went on. 'I don't *need* all these computers and comms and Vee and all the other stuff. They just don't feel *real* any more. Albion's real. And I'd rather be there than here.'

Winter frowned. 'There's Karma to consider. He thought you were a Spirit Childe; if you go back he'll still think it, and you'll run straight into trouble.'

'But I won't!' Angel's enthusiasm was growing. 'Not this time, because I'll go prepared. SynergyMed cured your illness with a couple of shots, and I can do the same in Albion. All I have to do is buy some medications and take them with me, and there'll be no more epidemics in your Village! Karma will think it's the Spirit Childe's magic, and everyone'll be happy!'

Winter wavered. The thought of being able to cure such illness as the Grey Rose sickness obviously excited him; but at the same time he was struggling to be scrupulously fair. 'But what about your mother?' he asked at last.

She shrugged. 'What about her? She's only interested in herself. You've seen how she revels in all this publicity and attention. It isn't for my sake; it's for her own.'

'She's been very kind to me,' Winter pointed out hesitantly.

'Oh, sure she has; because it's good for her image. I mean, it looks great, doesn't it – taking in a poor

Unparented boy out of the goodness of her heart, feeding him, clothing him, treating him like her own . . . You *bet* she's been kind. And it isn't costing her a single cred, because all the sponsors are paying for it, with plenty more on top! She doesn't actually *care* about you, Winter. And I don't think she really cares about me, either.'

She could see that her words had gone home. Winter didn't want to believe her – he probably felt guilty about it – but, deep down, he knew she was right. Soho was as transparent as plasglass. Winter wouldn't miss her.

And neither would Angel.

'The thing is,' she said, 'you're the only real friend I've ever had. And I don't want to lose you.'

He looked at her, a long, searching look, as if he was trying to decide whether or not he could – or dared – trust what she was proposing. Suddenly self-conscious, Angel turned her head away. Then after a minute, quietly, Winter spoke.

'I'm glad,' he said. 'Because you're the only real friend I've ever had, too.'

Twinkle came pattering in then. The Therapet's programme was still glitching from time to time, and she started to sing 'I'm Just A Little Funfriend' while turning round and round in circles. Angel picked her up and cuddled her (it seemed to be the best way to stop the glitches), and during the momentary diversion, the one problem that she and Winter hadn't addressed rose up like a spectre in her mind.

She sighed and said, 'We've forgotten one thing. It's all very well to talk about going back to Albion. But *how*?'

Winter gazed down at the floor, but the new moving-pattern carpet that Soho had had installed made him feel dizzy, so he looked up again. 'I've been asking myself about that, and there's only one answer. That mirror sculpture, in the Experience Mart. We've got to use that. It's the only way.'

'Winter, that's impossible! It's on full view in an exhibition; if we start messing around with it, we'll have Mart security crashing on us like a comet! Anyway,' she added ruefully, 'you know what happens if we even *try* to go anywhere public.'

He did. Newsdrones, agents, publicists, celeb-chasers — they were out there in force, just waiting for a sighting of the Audacious Abductees. One step into open territory and they'd be mobbed, and no face-make in the world was a good enough disguise.

Then abruptly something slotted in her mind. The arguments she had been having with Soho . . .

'Wait a min,' she said. 'I've got an idea . . .' It would be pure blackmail, but she didn't care. Soho used the same tactics when it suited her, so why not play her at her own game?

She looked at Winter again, and there was the ghost of a grin on her face.

'Wait till Soho comes home,' she said. 'And I'll see if I can fix this problem of ours . . .'

'A piece of art?' Soho looked at Angel in puzzlement. 'But darling, whatever do you want it *for*?'

Angel smiled her sweetest smile. 'It isn't *for* anything,

Soho. I just like it. And – and it's got a sort of – sentimental value.'

Ah; that snared Soho's interest. 'I don't *quite see*, darling,' she said cautiously. 'What do you mean?'

'Well . . . after Winter and I escaped, when we got to the Experience Mart – you know what happened; the way we both lost consciousness—'

'Of course, of course!' Soho had never doubted a word of the fict, even if it was full of convenient gaps and glaring logical holes.

'When we woke up, you see, that sculpture was the very first thing I saw.' Angel sighed. 'I'll never forget that moment, Soho. *Never.*' She paused for a significant moment, then delivered her final strike. 'I've never told anyone before; it seemed so silly. But it would mean a lot to me to have it. And maybe I could repay you in some way . . .?'

The arrow, as Angel Ravenhair would have said, struck right on target. Soho's eyes glinted thoughtfully and she said, 'That's *very* sweet of you, darling.' She sighed. 'You know, don't you, how hurt I feel by your attitude about the Vee-movie? The people are simply *pleading* for you to sign the contract, and it's *such* a wonderful deal . . .'

'Yes,' said Angel, hanging her head so that her mother wouldn't see her triumphant expression. 'I know, Soho. I've been silly, haven't I? So if I *could* have the sculpture . . .'

Soho swooped and hugged her. 'Darling, of course you shall have it! Wait here, now; wait *right* here, and I'll vid the Experience Mart this very min! What did you say the piece is called . . .?'

The sculpture was delivered the following morning. It came in one of the Mart's own express-autos, with two Mart staff and an Art Conceptualiser in attendance, and it was carefully set up, exactly as it had been at the exhibition, in the main activity room. Angel had wanted it in her own room, but Soho drew the line at that.

'No, no, darling; we must have it here, where everyone who comes can see it and hear the story. I've told Infax and W?W?W? about it, and they want to do a little piece for the main evening 'casts. Roma's coming this afternoon to get you ready – Oh, be CAREFUL, you men! Do mind that table; it's interactive and it cost a FORTUNE!'

Angel didn't argue the point. She had the sculpture, and that was enough. One mystery still remained, though. When Soho had begun negotiations to buy the piece, she had naturally assumed that the sculpture still belonged to its creator, who must be persuaded to sell it. But it didn't. In fact, neither the exhibition organisers nor anyone else knew who its creator was, and there was even some confusion over how it had been included in the exhibition in the first place. Soho was perfectly happy with that. With no one else to claim it, the piece was the property of the Experience Mart, and with the promise of some splendid publicity the Mart was only too delighted to sell it for a very favourable price.

So the sculpture was installed, and the mystery of its origin remained unsolved. Angel didn't know whether to be disappointed or relieved. On the one hand, she very much wanted to find out the truth about the mirror devices; where they had come from, why they had been

137

made; above all, of course, how they worked. But on the other hand, she was wise enough to realise that too much curiosity could lead to trouble. She and Winter had the sculpture; they had made it work once before and, she believed, could make it work again. Better to leave it at that and not probe too deeply.

They started to experiment as soon as they could, using every spare minute when Soho was out. Soho didn't go out that often, though, and the number of 'friends' who called at the apartment was also increasing. (Strange, Angel thought cynically, how many 'friends' had suddenly appeared on the scene now that they were all famous.) There were frustratingly few chances to work on the device, and after three days they were getting nowhere.

The problem was the same one that they had encountered in Albion: the number of possible angle combinations was so vast that hitting on the right one could take a lifetime. Again, Angel tried every mental trick she could think of to recall exactly how the mirrors had been set last time, but whenever she thought that she had cracked the conundrum, the door failed, yet again, to open.

One idea helped a little, and that was to programme every setting that they tried into Vee. It ensured that they didn't waste time by accidentally repeating the same settings – but beyond that small advantage it achieved nothing at all. The trouble was, as Angel said to Winter one evening when they had escaped together into Avalonne for a quiet talk, the angles had to be totally precise. It only took one mirror to be one zillionth of a degree out, and the result was a resounding zero – and that was to say nothing of the water jets; they had to be right, too. It was all starting to look hopeless.

'What I don't understand,' she said, picking a stem of Avalonne's clean, dry grass and twirling it between finger and thumb, 'is that we made it work last time.'

'I know.' Winter stared moodily out across the distant landscape, where a colossal but perfectly safe lightning storm was doing spectacular things to one of Angel's roseate sunsets. The storm was silent; thunder sound effects were too much of a distraction. 'Or rather, you did. I wasn't in much of a condition to do anything; I didn't even see you set it up.'

She nibbled the grass stem, which tasted like her favourite sweetstick. 'That's the weird thing. I'm not sure that I *did* set it up. I didn't tell you at the time — you weren't in much of a condition, like you said — but when we got into the cave and I saw the mirrors, they looked . . . different.'

'Different?'

'Yes. As if they'd . . . they'd been moved somehow. I was *sure* I hadn't left them that way.'

'You must have done.'

'I know. But . . .' She shrugged. 'I still can't get rid of the feeling that I didn't.'

Winter was quiet for a few moments, thoughtful. Then he sighed and shook his head. 'You must be mistaken, Angel. The mirrors can't possibly have moved by themselves.' He paused. 'Maybe something else shifted them; water dripping inside the cave, say.'

'Yes,' she said, hope sinking. 'Maybe.' Crazy to think that

the mirrors might have some magical property of their own. Magic might work in Avalonne, but not in the real world. Only people like the Albionites believed it could, and a fat lot of good it did them.

Suddenly the distant lightning storm froze in midflash, and a loud chime sounded from somewhere behind them. A bland, disembodied voice announced, 'House communications: personal visitor, security gate three.'

'Oh, flackers!' said Angel. 'Soho's out – I forgot to disable the interrupt.'

'Ignore it,' Winter suggested. 'They'll go away eventually.'

That was true; but a hostile little spark had lit up in Angel, triggered by her frustration. She was in exactly the right mood to tell some spidering 'friend' what they could do with their 'just happened to be in the district, sweetie' social call; it would relieve her tension and make her feel a *lot* better.

'No,' she said. 'I'll sort it. You wait here.'

Emerging from the Vee cubicle, she strode to the house console and slammed her first down on the winking comm light.

'Angel Ashe,' she snapped, in a voice reminiscent of Cray in one of his filthiest tempers. 'Who is it, and what do you want?'

The vidscreen had been playing up lately (probably wearing out from over-use), so the caller's face was blurry and distorted. All Angel could tell was that it was a man. She didn't think she had ever seen him before.

'Ah,' said a voice. 'Miss Ashe. The very person.'

Angel did a double-take. *Miss* Ashe? No one had used

that form of address for centuries! 'Er – yes,' she said, flummoxed. 'Who are you?'

'My name is—' But the comm link glitched and made a screeching noise at that moment, so the name wasn't audible. 'I need to talk to you, Miss Ashe. It's extremely important.'

A celeb–chaser. They always used that tactic, pretending they had some irresistible deal to offer, or that they were a long–lost relative. They must think she was short of a circuit or two, and Angel's ire rose.

'Sure,' she said with heavy sarcasm. 'It always is, isn't it? What's *your* fict – a world tour and a few million creds? Or are you another one of Winter's Prime Parents?'

The man at the gate made a noise that sounded like a growl. 'I assure you, Miss Ashe, I am not pretending to be anything! If you will just allow me to come to your apartment—'

'Pigs to that!' Angel snorted. 'Go and jump under a String car!'

She was about to thump the comm cutoff, but his voice forestalled her. '*Miss Ashe*! It's about the mirror sculpture!'

Angel hesitated as something stirred in her intuition. 'What about it?' she said uneasily.

'It's my—' *screee*! The link was playing up again.

'What did you say?' Angel shouted. 'What do you know about the sculpture?'

There was a pause. Then: 'I know everything about it, my dear young lady. I should. I made it.'

ELEVEN

Angel's garbled summons brought Winter running from the Vee cubicle, and they waited nervously for the man to arrive at the apartment, tracking the bubble-lift on the smaller vidscreen near the main aperture.

'There he is!' Angel pointed to the screen as the man got out of the lift on their floor.

Winter peered with narrowed eyes at the display, but the security cams didn't show much detail; just an indistinct figure hurrying along the corridor.

'He looks small,' Winter said uncertainly. 'And . . .'

But he didn't get any further, for at that moment the entry chime rang.

The man *was* small; no taller than Angel, though considerably wider, especially around the waist. She was also surprised to see that he was quite old, with a square, lined face and grey hair pulled into a jaunty tail on the top of his head. But it was his eyes that really startled her. One was hazel and the other grey, and the combination gave the bizarre illusion that the two of them worked independently of each other. She had never seen anything like it before; if it was a transplant, then it certainly was original.

The man, however, took little notice of Angel's appearance. His weird eyes merely raked her briefly up and down, and without bothering with greetings or other pleasantries he said,

'Miss Ashe, you have something of mine. And I want it back.'

He walked into the apartment without waiting for a reply, and, taken unawares, Angel stepped out of his path without realising it. Winter had backed away, too, and though he was behind her she could almost physically feel the tension radiating from him.

'Look,' she said, feigning a level of courage that, suddenly, she didn't feel, 'I don't know who in Tokyo you are, but if you think you can come here claiming that the sculpture's yours—where's your proof of ownership?'

'I don't need proof of ownership,' he said with weary patience. 'The artefact is mine, because I built it. End of story. And, as I said, I would like it back.'

'Now, *listen.*' Angel's temper had begun to fray. 'My Prime Parent bought the sculpture from the Experience Mart exhibition. The Mart people tried to trace the maker' (well, that was a bit of an exaggeration) 'but they couldn't, so legally it was theirs to sell. If you *did* make it, and you didn't want them to sell it, you shouldn't have put it in the show in the first place, should you?'

'My dear young lady—'

'Stop calling me that! It's patronising.'

He ignored her protest. 'My dear young lady, I did not put it in the show! Its inclusion was a mistake, don't you see? It shouldn't have been in that gallery, and it most *certainly* shouldn't have been sold! Now: I don't know how much your Prime Parent paid for it, though knowing these

Mart people I imagine she was grossly overcharged; but I assure you, I will recompense her in full, with an extra sum to make up for her – and your – inconvenience.' He beamed at Angel, which was quite an alarming experience, as he had no teeth whatsoever. 'There, now. I can't be fairer than that, can I?'

Angel looked quickly at Winter, but he didn't notice. He was staring fixedly at the man, and standing very, very still. The fact that he hadn't said a word, or backed her up in any way, annoyed Angel, and her mouth set in a hard line.

'Sorry,' she said ferociously. 'It isn't for resale.'

The beam faded and the colour of the stranger's grey eye became arctic. 'Miss Ashe,' he said, and there was a hint of menace in his tone now, 'please believe me when I tell you that I am *not* joking about this matter. The sculpture belongs to me, and I fully intend to claim it. I'd advise you, for your own sake, to stop being foolish and return it to me *at once*.'

Muscles worked in Angel's throat. 'Are you trying to threaten me?'

'I would much prefer not to. But if you won't take my advice . . .' He spread his hands. 'You'll leave me with no other choice.'

Angel wished Soho were here. She would have known what to do: she'd have thrown such a fit – and probably a few objects as well – that the man would have turned tail and bolted. Angel didn't have that streak in her, and the fact that Winter was just standing there and being a useless flea made things worse. Though she didn't want to admit it, she was more than a little frightened now. What if the man was a crazy? He could be dangerous; he might have a stun-detonator, or even something as horribly, dangerously basic as a knife . . .

'Look,' she said, moderating her voice to what she hoped was soothing, reassuring *nice*ness, 'I'm sure you don't really want to threaten me, and I'm sure there's no need for us to quarrel about this.'

The smile returned like the sun emerging from behind a cloud. 'Ah, *that*'s better. I knew when I set eyes on you that you were a sensible girl, and I agree absolutely. So: if you'll just show me where my property is—'

He had brushed past Angel before she could move a centi, and hurried – almost scurried – in the direction of the main room. 'Hey!' Angel shouted. 'Come back! You can't flit round my home as if you owned it!'

He took no notice, and when she ran after him she was just in time to see the main room's aperture closing behind him.

'*Hey!*' she yelled again. The aperture had only partly reopened as she charged through, and the membranes let out a protesting hiss. The man was in the main room, striding towards the mirror sculpture on its plinth. Angel's eyes widened as she saw him reach out and touch it; he gave a snort of annoyance, mumbling something like, 'All wrong, all *wrong*!' and his hands moved rapidly over the mirrors. That was the final straw. Angel thumbed her arm strip and shrieked, '*Security!*' with the full strength of her lungs.

The Whirligig came zooming into the room, bouncing

agitatedly and squawking, 'MESSAGE RELAYED! EMERGENCY ACCESS ACTIVATED! DON'T PANIC, ANGEL!'

'You silly young *fool!*' The man spun round from the sculpture, his eyes flaring and something like panic in *his* voice. 'You don't realise what you're doing!'

'Get out of this apartment!' Angel snarled. '*Now!*'

There was a crash and a pounding of feet near the main aperture, and a five-strong Azure Block security team appeared. They skidded to a halt when they saw that no one was actually being murdered yet, and the leader said breathlessly, 'What's the problem?'

'Him.' Angel pointed at the man, who had stepped away from the mirrors and was looking very defensive. 'He got in here under false pretences and – and—' But she didn't want to tell them the whole vid; if she did, it would get back to Soho, and Angel had enough to worry about without that.

'He's making a nuisance of himself,' she told the security leader. 'He conned me into believing he's a friend of my Prime Parent, but he's just another celeb-chaser.'

The guard nodded curtly. 'Understood.' And to the man, 'All right, chaser. You heard what Angel Ashe said.' A thumb jerked towards the aperture. 'Out.'

The man's cheeks puffed. 'You don't understand any more than she does! I am *not* a celeb-chaser; I simply—'

'*OUT,*' the security guard repeated. People didn't argue with that tone; it was one of the talents that had made him team leader. He glanced at Angel again. 'Do you want to claim trauma compensation? It's your right.'

Angel shook her head. 'No. Just get rid of him.'

Another efficient nod. 'Will do, Angel Ashe. And I'll log him on Recog, so if he comes back we'll be alerted straight away.'

'Yes,' she said. 'Thanks. Thanks double-A.'

She followed as they led the man to the main aperture. He had stopped protesting, realising that the odds were too stacked to argue with. But as the guards pushed him out into the corridor, he turned and gave Angel a last, penetrating look.

'I'm sorry for you,' he said. 'I thought you had more intelligence than you obviously have. Well, so be it. But I'll warn you now: you're involved in something that is far, far beyond your ability to understand. And if you're not very careful, you could come to regret what you're doing in a *very* big way!'

'That's enough!' One of the guards shook him warningly, and he didn't say any more. Only the look lingered for another moment. Then, abruptly, he broke the eye contact, and he and the guards were gone.

'Whooo . . .' Angel let out a long, harsh breath and leaned against the wall for a few moments, until her heart stopped thumping quite so savagely. Winter had vanished, but from the direction of his room she could hear Twinkle singing, 'Little Pink Flowers'. Twinkle's erratic programming had recently given her a stubborn compulsion to follow Winter around whenever she could, and this particular song was her way of trying to soothe people's jangled nerves. Angel's mouth pursed, and she headed for Winter's room.

He was sitting on the floor beside his crib, knees hunched up under his chin, eyes shut, and Twinkle still singing as she treadle-pawed his feet. He must have heard Angel come in, but he didn't react.

'Stop that din, Twinkle!' Angel ordered. She stood over Winter. 'Well?'

'I'm sorry.' His voice was not quite steady.

'Sorry?' she echoed. 'That's a spidering lot of use now, isn't it? Where were you – Planet Moron? Not saying a word, leaving me to deal with that crazy on my own—'

'He's not a crazy,' said Winter.

She stopped in mid-tirade. 'What do you mean?'

'What I said. He's not a crazy.' Winter opened his eyes at last and looked up at her. The only time she had seen his face so deadly serious was when the Grey Rose sickness had come to his Village. 'I know, because I've seen him before. In Albion.'

'You've *what*?' Angel dropped to her knees on the floor beside him, forgetting the presence of Twinkle, who skittered out of the way with a squeak. 'When? Why didn't you *say* so?'

'I didn't want to, not in front of him. Do you remember, I told you about a stranger who came to the Village a couple of years ago? The one Karma decided was an evil spirit?'

'You mean, that was *him*?'

Winter nodded. 'I know it was. You don't forget someone like that. And now he's here in your world.' He looked Angel in the eye. 'I think he was telling the truth. He *did* make the mirror devices, and he must know how to use them. He's a time traveller, Angel. And I'm scared of him.'

She sagged until she was sitting on the floor at his side. 'Do you think he recognised you?' she asked.

'No. I look different now, after all the things people have done with my clothes and hair. That's why I didn't say anything to you while he was here. I thought it might be better – for us – if he didn't know I'm from another world.'

Angel saw the sense in that. 'I wonder if he realises that I've used the device?' she said, half to herself.

'We can't be sure, can we? But I'd guess that it's likely.' He shivered, despite the warm, scented air currents breezing artificially through the room. 'And if he does, that makes him even more dangerous. What was it he said – that if we're not careful we're going to regret it?'

'Something like that.' Angel's eyes were dark with a mixture of fear and anger. 'Look,' she went on after a few moments, 'he's obviously trying to stop us from using the device again, and one failure won't put him off. He'll have another go soon, and next time he'll be a lot more devious about it.' *I would much prefer not to have to threaten you*, he had said. *But if you won't take my advice . . .* She didn't know what he might or might not be capable of, or how far he would be prepared to go. But a man who had solved the secret of time travel, and didn't want to share it, would probably stop at nothing. And he had the power and the skill to be not just a dangerous enemy but a deadly one.

Twinkle, who had been hiding under Winter's crib,

suddenly emerged and started to sing 'Little Pink Flowers' again. She positioned herself between the two of them and dithered confusedly, uncertain which of them was more in need of comfort. Angel picked the Therapet up and absent-mindedly stroked her – then suddenly she sprang to her feet, dumping Twinkle on the floor again, and strode across the room.

'Come on!' she said, glancing back as she reached the aperture.

'Come on where?' Winter was as confused as Twinkle. 'What are you going to do?'

'Take another look at that device!' Angel's eyes were glinting with excitement – for she had just remembered something that had happened in the moments before the security team's arrival. The old man had reached out to the sculpture, and before anyone could stop him he had started to tinker with it.

So what, in those few secs before he was stopped, had he done?

As she hurried to the activity room Twinkle ran after her, squeaking, 'Is this a new game, Angel? I like games, don't you?'

'It's no game,' she told the Therapet. And they couldn't afford to waste any time: Soho would be back soon, and there was no knowing when they would be alone again without her hovering around. Angel wasn't about to wait for that. The old man would be back, she was sure of it – and soon.

She explained to Winter in a few terse sentences, and was relieved that he didn't use up any precious minutes

150

arguing with her. One chance; just one. If her theory was right—

'Get the medications!' she told Winter. They had amassed a hoard of pills and potions that she hazarded would cure just about anything the Albionites had wrong with them; wouldn't do to leave them behind. He fetched them at a run, and Angel thought wildly: *Is there anything else? Anything I've forgotten?*

'Oh, *let's* play a game, Angel!' a little voice by her feet pleaded. 'I know one called "Dancing Dimples" – shall I tell you what to do?'

Hand midway to the device, Angel paused and looked down. Twinkle was gazing back at her with such a pleading look that her heart gave a lurch. *Oh, don't be ridiculous! It's an automaton, not a real animal!* 'Go away, Twinkle,' she said, more kindly than she had intended to. 'We're busy.'

Twinkle's shimmering whiskers trembled. 'Where are you going, Angel?' she asked. Angel's mind jolted back to her birthday party, the flight along the corridor, and the glimpse she had had, as the bubble-lift started to whisk her away, of a little gold-and-silver creature trotting haplessly after her and calling, '*Come back, Angel! Please, come back!*'

'Ohhh . . .' In a single, convulsive movement she bent down and scooped the Therapet into her arms. Winter began, 'What in the stars—' but she gave him such a look that he changed his mind about saying the rest. Draping Twinkle over her shoulder, she stared hard at the device. The mirror angles *were* different. In fact . . . in fact, she would have bet her entire allowance that they were set

151

exactly as they had been in the cave behind the waterfall . . .

She grasped hold of Winter's hand and gripped it with all her strength. 'Shut your eyes, if you want to,' she said.

'Angel, it might not work—'

'Don't think like that! *Will* it to work – *make* it work, come *on!*'

They stepped together towards the sculpture. The water jets played. Light reflected vividly in the plasglass surfaces. Then suddenly it seemed that all the mirrors lit up at once. For a disorientating moment Angel saw her own face, but multiplied a thousand times, stretching into infinity—

Twinkle let out a squawk that echoed round the room. Three seconds later the Whirligig skimmed in, lights dancing on its display, voice repeating excitedly, 'INQUIRY! INQUIRY! WHERE ARE YOU, ANGEL? WHERE ARE YOU, ANGEL?'

But there was no one in the apartment to give the Whirligig an answer.

Coming Soon . . .

MIRROR MIRROR PART II:

RUNNING FREE

Louise Cooper

The gripping sequel to *BREAKING THROUGH* . . .

Having made it back to her own time with her new friend, Winter, Angel Ashe is faced with a frightening challenge.

The mirror sculpture, which now belongs to Angel, turns out to have a previous owner – Pye – and he wants it back. But there's no way Angel will give it up – not now that she's discovered the secret to time-travel. But will Pye – a veteran time traveller himself – want these two young novices messing with his sculpture, as they learn how to skip through the parallel universe?

Angel and Winter cannot begin to realise the danger they face, but they are sure of one thing – nothing on *earth* is going to stop them now . . .